THE REAL
LIFE OF
SEBASTIAN
KNIGHT

BY VLADIMIR NABOKOV

AVAILABLE FROM NEW DIRECTIONS

Laughter in the Dark

Nikolai Gogol

The Real Life of Sebastian Knight

THE REAL LIFE OF SEBASTIAN KNIGHT

VLADIMIR NABOKOV

INTRODUCTION BY MICHAEL DIRDA

A NEW DIRECTIONS BOOK

The author wishes to acknowledge his debt to Mme. Lucy Léon and to Professor Agnes Perkins of Wellesley College, both of whom read and emended *The Real Life of Sebastian Knight* in manuscript.

Manufactured in the United States of America
First published clothbound by New Directions in 1949 and reissued clothbound in 1959. First paperbound edition (NDP432) published in 1977 and reissued (NDP1107) with an Introduction by Michael Dirda in 2008.

Library of Congress Cataloging-in-Publication Data

Nabokov, Vladimir Vladimirovich, 1899-1977.
  The real life of Sebastian Knight / Vladimir Nabokov ; introduction by
Michael Dirda.
     p. cm.
   ISBN 978-0-8112-1750-7 (alk. paper)
  1. Novelists--Fiction. 2. Knight, Sebastian (Fictitious
character)—Fiction. I. Title.
   PS3527.A15R4 2008
   813'.54—dc22
                          2008019249

10 9 8 7 6 5 4

NEW DIRECTIONS BOOKS ARE PUBLISHED FOR JAMES LAUGHLIN
BY NEW DIRECTIONS PUBLISHING CORPORATION,
80 EIGHTH AVENUE, NEW YORK 10011

INTRODUCTION

INTRODUCTION

by Michael Dirda

BY THE LATE 1930s, the Russian émigré novelist who published under the pen name V. Sirin recognized that it was time to leave Paris. The spreading power of Nazism had already driven him—and his Jewish wife Véra—out of Berlin, where they and many other Russians had settled after the Bolshevik Revolution. But where to go next?

As a young man, Vladimir Nabokov—to give his real name—had spent three years as a Cambridge University undergraduate; he spoke excellent English. But nothing much came of his attempts to find lecturing opportunities or appropriate employment in Britain. So in May of 1940, the forty-one-year-old writer, his wife, and their young son Dmitri took ship for the United States. There he would eventually publish in *The New Yorker*, teach at Wellesley and Cornell, and one day become world-famous as the author of *Lolita*.

But those achievements were years in the future. Shortly before leaving France, when he didn't yet know where he would end up, Nabokov set to work on a new novel, one composed not in his beloved Russian, but for the first time directly in English. As his biographer Brian Boyd writes:

"With Dmitri playing or asleep in the one main room of their apartment, Nabokov had to retreat into the bathroom to write, using a suitcase over the bidet as a desk. When the sun went down the room quickly chilled and his fingers would grow numb from the cold and the long hours of writing. The whole time he spent on the novel he was oppressed by the knowledge that his mother had fallen seriously ill and that Hitler's tightening grip on Czechoslovakia made it impossible for him to visit her. And he had to compose the novel not in his special Russian but in what he felt was a second-rate brand of English. Despite the circumstances, he wrote on unflinchingly. A British literary competition for which he wanted to enter the novel required manuscripts to be received in London by the end of January 1939. On January 29 he reported to a friend that he had finished the book and dispatched it."

When *The Real Life of Sebastian Knight* finally appeared—in America, from New Directions, on December 18, 1941— Nabokov wrote to one Russian acquaintance that he regarded it as a tour de force.

Sebastian Knight is a scion of an aristocratic Russian family who flees the Revolution with his stepmother and half-brother, attends Cambridge, adopts his English mother's maiden name, and becomes a critically esteemed novelist. Following the writer's premature death at the age of thirty-six, his six-years younger brother— known only as V. — almost immediately decides to start gathering material for a biography. Thus the novel comprises V.'s childhood memories of Sebastian, a series of interviews with people who were close to the writer, and brief summaries of his five books, sometimes with extensive quotation. Throughout, the rather colorless and bumbling V. seeks almost desperately to grasp the essence of his brother's life, his real life.

In one sense, this is obviously impossible, a fact neatly underscored by the leitmotif of mistaken identity. Sebastian, for example, visits Roquebrune where his flighty English mother had lived and vividly imagines her spectral presence—and later discovers he was at the wrong Roquebrune. V. encounters a mysterious detective named Mr. Silbermann—and fails to recognize that he is the avatar (or original) of Mr. Siller, even though the latter is supposedly "the most alive of Sebastian's creatures." (104) A coquettish Frenchwoman, a hospital patient, perhaps even V. himself, are not what they at first seem to be. So how do we distinguish the real from the false, the authentic from the apparent?

Such questions lie at the heart of Nabokovian fiction, a fiction full of ambiguity, traps for the unwary, camouflaged clues, tongue-in-cheek parody, and dizzying paradoxes. Read *Lolita* for the first time, and the identity of Humbert Humbert's adversary arrives as a shock. Where did this guy come from? But reread the book and you can see how his sly presence pervades the text from the very beginning. "Every contact," notes a standard manual on police practice, "leaves traces." One just needs to know where to look and how. A good reader must be a textual detective, trust no one, and regard every sentence as masking a secret or a secret agenda. Nabokov once likened his narrative esthetic to those old pictorial puzzles in which children are asked by a jolly, pipe-smoking old salt to discover a sailboat, a yellow pencil, a pokey little puppy, and a host of other objects scattered throughout a busy and crowded seaside picture. Find what the sailor has hidden.

So what will the attentive reader find in *The Real Life of Sebastian Knight*? To begin with, a certain amount of autobiography. In the most obvious sense, Sebastian might be a partial portrait of the artist as a young man, Nabokov's equivalent of Joyce's Stephen Dedalus. Creator and subject share the same birth year and attend the same university;

Sebastian's companion, Clare Bishop, is said to recall Véra Nabokov (as perhaps does the kind and generous Helene Grinstein). The major crisis of Sebastian's sentimental life must certainly owe something to Nabokov's experience during his tormented love affair with Irina Guadanini. Though not a roman à clef, this novel reveals an artist transmuting the inchoate materials of his own life into a shaped and complex narrative of great beauty. Through his mouthpiece V., Nabokov actually comments on the autobiographical elements of his novel:

"The light of personal truth is hard to perceive in the shimmer of an imaginary nature, but what is still harder to understand is the amazing fact that a man writing of things which he really felt at the time of writing, could have had the power to create simultaneously—and out of the very things which distressed his mind—a fictitious and faintly absurd character." (114)

In one way, then, Sebastian's real life might simply be Nabokov's imaginary one, a thought-experiment, an almost Borges-like exploration of a forking path not actually taken: This is what I would have been like had I become a "faintly absurd" English novelist.

Not precisely hidden, though possibly underappreciated, are the novel's atmospheric vignettes: scenes of old Russia, romantic Paris between the wars, rain-swept Cambridge. These imbue *The Real Life of Sebastian Knight* with a distinct period feel, one reminiscent of so many grainy, shadowy 1930s black-and-white films. Like the naïve Peter Lorre in the *The Mask of Dimitrios* (who searches half of Europe for the truth about a master spy), the unsophisticated V. travels from England to Switzerland to Germany to France in his quest for the identity of the elusive femme fatale who wrecked his brother's life.

In that quest Nabokov's book carries us into the world of university dons and elegant cocottes, into the tiny apartments where former millionaires pass tedious afternoons playing chess in their shirtsleeves, and into the receiving rooms of slightly seedy French country estates. Everyone travels by express train or hired car. The hotel lobbies are unwelcoming, the air smoky or dank, and Europe feels more than a little timeworn and wistful.

Moreover, an atmosphere of the valedictory haunts *The Real Life of Sebastian Knight*. It is a book about farewells—and the difficulty of farewells, and even the possibility that final farewells might not be forever. V. cannot bear to think that his brother is truly gone—and convinces himself that Sebastian's ghost may be guiding him on his biographical quest. The young Sebastian, we learn, never ate the violet candies his frivolous English mother gave him when they met for a last time: The candies, and the English language, represented his only legacy from her—apart from a comfortable income. (She is also associated with the color violet, the hue of decadence, and as Nabokov revealed in a much later Cornell lecture, "the very color of time.") The many references to Russian as more nuanced and musical than English remind us how much Nabokov suffered himself in saying goodbye to his native language.

Whatever else it does, then, *The Real Life of Sebastian Knight* beautifully evokes shabby elegance, heartache, and weary desperation. As Michael Wood notes, "this novel's deepest mood is what Nabokov elsewhere calls that of the preterist: a longing for lost treasures, tastes, languages, countries, loved ones, a hope that they may be magically stored some-where because they *cannot* have vanished, simply gone like smoke." V. says something similar about the love between Clare and Sebastian: "And it is hard to believe that the warmth, the tenderness, the beauty of it has not been gath-ered, and is not treasured somewhere, somehow, by some immortal witness of mortal life." (87) In one sense, art cer-tainly makes the transitory timeless, but there lurks a dis-tinct transcendental yearning in that statement. Perhaps the created world, like art, is also a realm of extra dimensions, secret handshakes, unnoticed patterns in the carpet. There may be, to adopt one of Sebastian's phrases, "an aetiological secret" (96) to seemingly "aleatory occurrences." (96) More on this in a moment.

Suffused by a Depression grayness, the novel evokes every past as an enchanted realm, a lost paradise, bathed in sunshine. One old lady's "dry account cannot convey to the untravelled reader the implied delights of a winter day such as she describes in St. Petersburg; the pure luxury of a cloudless sky designed not to warm the flesh, but solely to please the eye; the sheen of sledge-cuts on the hard-beaten snow of spacious streets with a tawny tinge about the mid-dle tracks due to a rich mixture of horse-dung; the brightly coloured bunch of toy-balloons hawked by an aproned ped-lar; the soft curve of a cupola, its gold dimmed by the bloom of powdery frost; the birch trees in the public gardens, every tiniest twig outlined in white; the rasp and tinkle of winter traffic . . ." (5-6)

When Sebastian goes up to Cambridge in 1919, he finds himself entering a cozy, almost Sherlockian England:

"A real hansom-cab took him from the station to Trinity

College: the vehicle, it seemed, had been waiting there especially for him, desperately holding out against extinction till that moment, and then gladly dying out to join side whiskers and the Large Copper. The slush of streets gleaming wet in the misty darkness with its promised counterpoint—a cup of strong tea and a generous fire—formed a harmony which somehow he knew by heart. The pure chimes of tower-clocks, now hanging over the town, now overlapping and echoing afar, in some odd, deeply familiar way blended with the piping cries of the newspaper vendors. And as he entered the stately gloom of Great Court with gowned shadows passing in the mist and the porter's bowler hat bobbing in front of him, Sebastian felt that he somehow recognised every sensation, the wholesome reek of dark turf, the ancient sonority of stone slabs under heel, the blurred outlines of dark walls overhead—everything."(43)

Few modern writers can match Nabokov at such evocative mood-music. While brightening and advancing the story, these descriptions also display Nabokov's characteristic lexical precision and that slightly old-fashioned formality that sometimes verges on aristocratic hauteur. Yet, turn a page, and his prose can be as simple and laconic as anything found in a detective-story magazine. At one point in his quest V. stops in Berlin:

"Large wet snowflakes were drifting aslant the Passauer Strasse in West-Berlin as I approached an ugly old house, its face half-hidden in a mask of scaffolding. I tapped on the glass of the porter's lodge, a muslin curtain was roughly drawn aside, a small window was knocked open and a blowsy old woman gruffly informed me that Frau Helene

Grinstein did live in the house. I felt a queer little shiver of elation and went up the stairs. 'Grinstein,' said a brass plate on the door.

"A silent boy in a black tie with a pale swollen face let me in and without so much as asking my name, turned and walked down the passage. There was a crowd of coats on the rack in the tiny hall. A bunch of snow-wet chrysanthemums lay on the table between two solemn top hats. As no one seemed to come, I knocked at one of the doors, then pushed it open and then shut it again. I had caught a glimpse of a dark-haired little girl, lying fast asleep on a divan, under a moleskin coat." (134)

Philip Marlowe, Sam Spade—is that you?

What else is hidden in *The Real Life of Sebastian Knight*? For its many admirers, the novel itself is one of Nabokov's hidden masterpieces—"absolutely enchanting," according to Edmund Wilson, "beguiling and melancholy" in the words of Julian Moynahan. Its early fans included such distinguished writers as Flannery O'Connor and Howard Nemerov (who once hoped to model his own literary career after Sebastian Knight's). Nabokov scholar Charles Nicol tellingly observed that the book was "more congenially designed for rereading than any novel I know." Of course, it doesn't just invite rereadings, it needs them.

True, there was a time when *The Real Life of Sebastian Knight* was occasionally viewed as "Nabokov for beginners," or even as a pallid trial version of *Pale Fire*: Charles Kinbote's commentary on the poetry and life of John Shade is certainly similar to V.'s inquiry into the past and art of Sebastian Knight. Secret Sharers all. Yet while *Pale Fire* is blatantly tricky—providing a headspinning series of trapdoors and false bottoms, replete with doublings and doubts—*Sebastian Knight* only seems simple on a first read-through. The novel's final pages, in particular, cast a retrospective shadow over all that has gone before.

On the surface, *The Real Life of Sebastian Knight* chronicles the obstacles and detours confronting a would-be literary biographer—rather like a novelistic reworking of A.J.A. Symons' then recent, and groundbreaking, *The Quest for Corvo* (1934). V. cleans out his brother's apartment, talks with Sebastian's closest undergraduate friend, visits the novelist's former secretary, and tries to speak with Clare Bishop. At the same time, he deftly interlaces anecdotes about Sebastian's life, keeps us aware of his own views and frustrations, and periodically pauses to discuss the various novels: *The Prismatic Bezel*, for example, examines the nature of identity against the backdrop of a classic country-house murder mystery; *Success* chronicles how a dogged Fate eventually brings together two intended lovers.

Sebastian's close college friend notes that for a writer "reality" is "a turmoil of words and fancies, uncomplete fancies and insufficient words." (50) In many ways, *The Real Life of Sebastian Knight* keeps the reader puzzled or amused about just such "uncomplete fancies and insufficient words." V.—who was educated in France and lives there—has oddly enough chosen to compose his book in English, a rather sophisticated English, which he nonetheless dismisses as "thin" and artificially acquired. The quotations from Mr. Goodman's *Tragedy of Sebastian Knight*—which faults a largely 1920s novelist for his refusal to engage with 1930s-style politics and social issues—provides a delicious compendium of kitschy criticism: "The 'ivory tower' cannot be suffered unless it is transformed into a lighthouse or a broadcasting station . . . In such an age . . . brimming with burning problems when . . . economic depression. . . . dumped . . . cheated . . . the man in the street . . . the growth of totalitarian . . . unemployment . . . the next super-great war . . . new aspects of family life . . . sex . . . structure of the universe." (117) Though this is funny, a nagging question remains: Just how good a novelist is Sebastian Knight really? V. regards him as the creator of masterpieces. But one critic claims the writer was dull at his best; another that a book's "fun seemed to me obscure and its obscurities funny." (86) A casual acquaintance of V. confesses that *Lost Property* and *The Prismatic Bezel* left him "puzzled and cross." (181) Periodically, Sebastian displays some of Nabokov's own occasional artistic faults—preciousness, for instance, and coldness and a kind of haughty condescension. His plots, too, have been dismissed as cutesy or pretentious. In Sebastian's apparent masterpiece, *The Doubtful Asphodel*, "a man is dying, and he is the hero of the tale . . . The man is the book; the book itself is heaving and dying, and drawing up a ghostly knee." (175) This may sound more ghastly than ghostly.

As nobody's life can ever be quite pinned down and we remain conundrums even to ourselves, so is *The Real Life of Sebastian Knight* swirling with mysteries that can't really be easily solved, or solved at all: Nabokov merely supplies the materials and then allows each reader to construct for himself "the real life of Sebastian Knight." As Sebastian writes, "It is not the parts that matter, it is their combinations." (176) (In chess, combinations are strategies, forcing a certain development. Perhaps here is one explanation for the chess references scattered throughout the book: Knight, Bishop, St. Damier—chessboard, in French. Even *roquer*, as in Roquebrune, means to castle.) The aware reader recognizes that reality is never just there, unmediated, but is always refracted, personalized. An old Swiss governess imagines Sebastian as an enchanted prince, V. regards him as a great writer, Clare Bishop first viewed him a doomed man and later thought he'd lost his mind, another woman dismisses him as a tedious and rather pathetic lover, Mr. Goodman calls him a literary snob out of touch with the times. Is the "real" Sebastian the sensitive soul who refuses to cut a beggar or the man given to cruel practical jokes or the pampered artiste who will deliberately humiliate the woman who loves him? Perhaps the ideal reader of this novel should possess Keats's "Negative Capability" and remain capable of, indeed positively enjoy "being in uncertainties, Mysteries, doubts without any irritable reaching after fact & reason."

Throughout the text, for instance, little flourishes regularly cast doubt even on the very existence of one or the other brother. Why is V. not given a name? We learn almost nothing of his background or life. Mr. Goodman, the writer's secretary and first biographer, never even knew that Sebastian had a brother. V. himself says that he would sometimes annoy Sebastian "merely as a wistful and vain attempt to make him notice my existence." (16) Note the word "vain." Could Sebastian be the creator of V.? Or vice versa? Remember that Sebastian's last projected novel was to be a "fictitious biography." (40) Perhaps this is it. To further complicate matters, we are even told repeatedly that "the only real number is one, the rest are mere repetition." (105) Two half brothers would make one whole person. Could other characters be equally insubstantial or illusory? Nina de Rechnoy's first husband says, "I often catch myself thinking that she has never existed" (147) and V. refers to his quest for Sebastian's unknown mistress as his "clumsy efforts to hunt down a ghost." (158)

Above all, there lingers the literally haunting question of ghosts, especially Sebastian's ghost. Should the abundant hints that Sebastian's spirit is directing V. in his quest be taken as poetic metaphor—that his brother lives on in V.'s soul and imagination—or should they be taken as indicating actual fact? Nabokov himself believed in a spectral "other world" (*potustoronmost* in Russian). In 1979 Véra Nabokov revealed that the other world was her husband's "main theme" and that it "saturates everything he wrote." Lecturing in the year that *Sebastian Knight* was published, Nabokov suggested "that human life is but a first installment of the serial soul and that one's individual secret is not lost in the process of earthly dissolution." Even the worldly Madame Lecerf says that some people "held special views about death that excluded hysterics." (156)

So then is the "real life" of Sebastian Knight his "afterlife"? Notice that when V. burns his brother's letters he happens to remark a few words on a page just before they go up in flame: "thy manner always to find." (38) "Thy" must refer to Sebastian, since the letters are to him. What do the words mean? In Nabokov's most famous story about a spectral afterlife, "The Vane Sisters," we read: "Anything that happened to Cynthia, after a given person had died, would be, she said, in the manner and mood of that person . . . it might be a string of minute incidents . . . the main thing was that its source could be identified. It was like walking though a person's soul, she said." Certainly, V. often feels a comparable spiritual identity with his brother:

"I daresay Sebastian and I also had some kind of common rhythm; this might explain the curious 'it-has-happened-before-feeling' which seizes me when following the bends of his life. And if, as often was the case with him, the 'whys' of his behaviour were as many X's, I often find their meaning disclosed now in a subconscious turn of this or that sentence put down by me." (34)

Is Sebastian guiding V's writing hand? This might account for the brilliance of his French-educated brother's English. Certainly, V.'s peregrinations repeat and echo scenes from Sebastian's novels. In summarizing the plot of *The Doubtful Asphodel*, V. notes, "We follow the gentle old chess player Schwarz, who sits down on a chair in a room in a house, to teach an orphan boy the moves of the knight; we meet the fat Bohemian woman with that grey streak showing in the fast colour of her cheaply dyed hair; we listen to a pale wretch noisily denouncing the policy of oppression to an attentive plainclothes man in an ill-famed public-house. The lovely tall primadonna steps in her haste into a puddle, and her silver shoes are ruined. An old man sobs and is soothed by a soft-lipped girl in mourning. Professor Nussbaum, a Swiss scientist, shoots his young mistress and himself dead in a hotel-room at half past three in the morning." (175) V. encounters parallels to all these characters.

But, if Sebastian's spook directs or even dictates the action, shouldn't his ghostly presence be felt? It is. V. often refers to his brother's shade as watching or overhearing him. "For a moment I seemed to see a transparent Sebastian at his desk." (39) Recall the mysterious Voice in the Mist; the cat that acts strangely when Sebastian is being discussed; what looks like the writer's cane left leaning against a garden bench. "Time and space," we are pointedly told, "were to him measures of the same eternity." (66) Besides, writes V. with enigmatic import, "what you are told is really three-fold: shaped by the teller, reshaped by the listener, concealed from both by the dead man of the tale." (52) To this one might add an observation from the novel's closing pages: "the soul is but a manner of being—not a constant state—that any soul may be yours, if you find and follow its undulations." (204) Any attentive reader can thus become, must become, Sebastian Knight. Through the reader who opens this book Sebastian finds the only "real life" he will ever know.

The Real Life of Sebastian Knight never won that British literary competition and wasn't published until Harry Levin and Delmore Schwartz recommended it to James Laughlin at New Directions. Nabokov's advance was only $150, but it began his real career in the United States. Alas, the book appeared just two weeks after Pearl Harbor, and the sales were modest. People, after all, had other matters on their minds besides novels written by authors with strange, foreign names. But that would gradually change. *The Real Life of Sebastian Knight* would eventually live again.

THE REAL
LIFE OF
SEBASTIAN
KNIGHT

THE REAL LIFE OF SEBASTIAN KNIGHT

SEBASTIAN KNIGHT was born on the thirty-first of December, 1899, in the former capital of my country. An old Russian lady who has for some obscure reason begged me not to divulge her name, happened to show me in Paris the diary she had kept in the past. So uneventful had those years been (apparently) that the collecting of daily details (which is always a poor method of self-preservation) barely surpassed a short description of the day's weather; and it is curious to note in this respect that the personal diaries of sovereigns—no matter what troubles beset their realms—are mainly concerned with the same subject. Luck being what it is when left alone, here I was offered something which I might never have hunted down had it been a chosen quarry. Therefore I am able to state that the morning of Sebastian's birth was a fine windless one, with twelve degrees (Reaumur) below zero . . . this is all, however, that the good lady found worth setting down. On second thought I cannot see any real necessity of complying with her anonymity. That she will ever read this book seems wildly improbable. Her name was and is Olga Olegovna Orlova—an egg-like alliteration which it would have been a pity to withhold.

Her dry account cannot convey to the untravelled reader the implied delights of a winter day such as she describes in St. Petersburg; the pure luxury of a cloudless sky designed not to warm the flesh, but solely to please the eye; the sheen of sledge-cuts on the hard-beaten snow of spacious streets with a tawny tinge about the middle tracks due to a rich mixture of horse-dung; the brightly coloured bunch of toy-balloons hawked by an aproned pedlar; the soft curve of a cupola, its gold dimmed by the bloom of powdery frost; the birch trees in the public gardens, every tiniest twig outlined in white; the rasp and tinkle of winter traffic . . . and by the way how queer it is when you look at an old picture postcard (like the one I have placed on my desk to keep the child of memory amused for a moment) to consider the haphazard way Russian cabs had of turning whenever they liked, anywhere and anyhow, so that instead of the straight, self-conscious stream of modern traffic one sees—on this painted photograph—a dream-wide street with droshkies all awry under incredibly blue skies, which, farther away, melt automatically into a pink flush of mnemonic banality.

I have not been able to obtain a picture of the house where Sebastian was born, but I know it well, for I was born there myself, some six years later. We had the same father: he had married again, soon after divorcing Sebastian's mother. Oddly enough, this second marriage is not mentioned at all in Mr. Goodman's *Tragedy of Sebastian Knight* (which appeared in 1936 and to which I shall have occasion to refer more fully); so that to readers of Goodman's book I am bound to appear non-existent—a bogus relative, a garrulous impostor; but Sebastian himself in his most autobiographical work (*Lost Property*) has some kind words to say about my mother—and I think she deserved them well. Nor is it exact, as suggested in the British press after Sebastian's decease, that his father was killed in the duel he fought in 1913; as a matter of fact he was steadily recovering from the bullet-wound in his chest, when—a full month later—he contracted a cold with which his half-healed lung could not cope.

A fine soldier, a warm-hearted, humorous, high-spirited man, he had in him that rich strain of adventurous restlessness which Sebastian inherited as a writer. Last winter at a literary lunch, in South Kensington, a celebrated old critic, whose brilliancy and learning I have always admired, was heard to remark as the talk fluttered around Sebastian Knight's untimely death: "Poor Knight! he really had two periods, the first—a dull man writing broken English, the second—a broken man writing dull English." A nasty dig, nasty in more ways than one for it is far too easy to talk of a dead author behind the backs of his books. I should like to believe that the jester feels no pride in recalling this particular jest, the more so as he showed far greater restraint when reviewing Sebastian Knight's work a few years ago.

Nevertheless, it must be admitted that in a certain sense, Sebastian's life, though far from being dull, lacked the terrific vigour of his literary style. Every time I open one of his books, I seem to see my father dashing into the room,—that special way he had of flinging open the door and immediately pouncing upon a thing he wanted or a creature he loved. My first impression of him is always a breathless one of suddenly soaring up from the floor, one half of my toy train still dangling from my hand and the crystal pendants of the chandelier dangerously near my head. He would bump me down as suddenly as he had snatched me up, as suddenly as Sebastian's prose sweeps the reader off his feet, to let him drop with a shock into the gleeful bathos of the next wild paragraph. Also some of my father's favourite quips seem to have broken into fantastic flower in such typical Knight stories as *Albinos in*

Black or *The Funny Mountain*, his best one perhaps, that beautifully queer tale which always makes me think of a child laughing in its sleep.

It was abroad, in Italy as far as I know, that my father, then a young guardsman on leave, met Virginia Knight. Their first meeting was connected with a fox-hunt in Rome, in the early nineties, but whether this was mentioned by my mother or whether I subconsciously recall seeing some dim snapshot in a family album, I cannot say. He wooed her long. She was the daughter of Edward Knight, a gentleman of means; this is all I know of him, but from the fact that my grandmother, an austere and wilful woman (I remember her fan, her mittens, her cold white fingers) was emphatically opposed to their marriage, and would repeat the legend of her objections even after my father had been married again, I am inclined to deduce that the Knight family (whatever it was) did not quite reach the standard (whatever that standard might have been) which was required by the redheels of the old regime in Russia. I am not sure either whether my father's first marriage did not clash somehow with the traditions of his regiment,—anyway his real military success only began with the Japanese war, which was after his wife had left him.

I was still a child when I lost my father; and it was very much later, in 1922, a few months before my mother's last and fatal operation, that she told me several things which she thought I should know. My father's first marriage had not been happy. A strange woman, a restless reckless being—but not my father's kind of restlessness. His was a constant quest which changed its object only after having attained it. Hers was a half-hearted pursuit, capricious and rambling, now swerving wide off the mark, now forgetting it midway, as one forgets one's umbrella in a taxicab. She was fond of my father after a fashion, a fitful fashion to say the least, and when one day it occurred to her that she might be in love with another (whose name my father never learnt from her lips), she left husband and child as suddenly as a rain-drop starts to slide tipwards down a syringa leaf. That upward jerk of the forsaken leaf, which had been heavy with its bright burden, must have caused my father fierce pain; and I do not like to dwell in mind upon that day in a Paris hotel, with Sebastian aged about four, poorly attended by a puzzled nurse, and my father locked up in his room, "that special kind of hotel room which is so perfectly fit for the staging of the worst tragedies: a dead burnished clock (the waxed moustache of ten minutes to two) under its glass dome on an evil mantelpiece, the French window with its fuddled fly between muslin and pane, and a sample of the hotel's letter paper on the well-used blotting-pad." This is a quotation from *Albinos in Black*, textually in no way connected with that special disaster, but retaining the distant memory of a child's fretfulness on a bleak hotel carpet, with nothing to do and a queer expansion of time, time gone astray, asprawl . . .

War in the Far East allowed my father that happy activity which helped him—if not to forget Virginia—at least to make life worth living again. His vigorous egotism was but a form of manly vitality and as such wholly consistent with an essentially generous nature. Permanent misery, let alone self-destruction, must have seemed to him a mean business, a shameful surrender. When in 1905 he married again, he surely felt satisfaction at having got the upper hand in his dealings with destiny.

Virginia reappeared in 1908. She was an inveterate traveller, always on the move and alike at home in any small pension or expensive hotel, home only meaning to her the comfort of constant change; from her, Sebastian inherited that strange, almost romantic, passion for sleeping-cars and Great European Express Trains, "the soft crackle of polished panels in the blue-shaded night, the long sad sigh of brakes at dimly surmised stations, the upward slide of an embossed leather blind disclosing a platform, a man wheeling luggage, the milky globe of a lamp with a pale moth whirling around it; the clank of an invisible hammer testing wheels; the gliding move into darkness; the passing glimpse of a lone woman touching silver-bright things in her travelling-case on the blue plush of a lighted compartment."

She arrived by the Nord Express on a winter day, without the slightest warning, and sent a curt note asking to see her son. My father was away in the country on a bear-hunt; so my mother quietly took Sebastian to the Hotel d'Europe where Virginia had put up for a single afternoon. There, in the hall, she saw her husband's first wife, a slim, slightly angular woman, with a small quivering face under a huge black hat. She had raised her veil above her lips to kiss the boy, and no sooner had she touched him than she burst into tears, as if Sebastian's warm tender temple was the very source and satiety of her sorrow. Immediately afterwards she put on her gloves and started to tell my mother in bad French a pointless and quite irrelevant story about a Polish woman who had attempted to steal her vanity-bag in the dining-car. Then she thrust into Sebastian's hand a small parcel of sugar-coated violets, gave my mother a nervous smile and followed the porter who was carrying out her luggage. This was all, and next year she died.

It is known from a cousin of hers, H. F. Stainton, that during the last months of her life she roamed all over the South of France, staying for a day or two at small hot provincial towns, rarely visited by tourists—feverish, alone (she had abandoned her lover) and probably very unhappy. One might think she was fleeing from someone or something, as she doubled and re-crossed her tracks; on the other hand, to any one who knew her moods, that hectic dashing might seem but a final exaggeration of her usual restlessness. She died of heart-failure (Lehmann's disease) at the little town of Roquebrune, in the summer of 1909. There was some difficulty in getting the body dispatched to England; her people had died some time before; Mr. Stainton alone attended her burial in London.

My parents lived happily. It was a quiet and tender union, unmarred by the ugly gossip of certain relatives of ours who whispered that my father, although a loving husband, was attracted now and then by other women. One day, about Christmas, 1912, an acquaintance of his, a very charming and thoughtless girl, happened to mention as they walked down the Nevsky, that her sister's fiancé, a certain Palchin, had known his first wife. My father said he remembered the man,—they had met at Biarritz about ten years ago, or was it nine . . .

"Oh, but he knew her later too," said the girl, "you see he confessed to my sister that he had lived with Virginia after you parted . . . Then she dropped him somewhere in Switzerland . . . Funny, nobody knew."

"Well," said my father quietly, "if it has not leaked out before, there is no reason for people to start prattling ten years later."

By a very grim coincidence, on the very next day, a good friend of our family, Captain Belov, casually asked my father whether it was true that his first wife came from Australia,— he, the Captain, had always thought she was English. My father replied that, as far as he knew, her parents had lived for some time in Melbourne, but that she had been born in Kent.

" . . . What makes you ask me that?" he added.

The Captain answered evasively that his wife had been at a party or something where somebody had said something . . .

"Some things will have to stop, I'm afraid," said my father.

Next morning he called upon Palchin, who received him with a greater show of geniality than was necessary. He had spent many years abroad, he said, and was glad to meet old friends.

"There is a certain dirty lie being spread," said my father without sitting down, "and I think you know what it is."

"Look here, my dear fellow," said Palchin, "no use my pretending I don't see what you are driving at. I am sorry people have been talking, but really there is no reason to lose our tempers . . . It is nobody's fault that you and I were in the same boat once."

"In that case, Sir," said my father, "my seconds will call on you."

Palchin was a fool and a cad, this much at least I gathered from the story my mother told me (and which in her telling had assumed the vivid direct form I have tried to retain here). But just because Palchin was a fool and a cad, it is hard for me to understand why a man of my father's worth should have risked his life to satisfy—what? Virginia's honour? His own desire of revenge? But just as Virginia's honour had been irredeemably forfeited by the very fact of her flight, so all ideas of vengeance ought to have long lost their bitter lust in the happy years of my father's second marriage. Or was it merely the naming of a name, the seeing of a face, the sudden grotesque sight of an individual stamp upon what had been a tame faceless ghost? And taken all in all was it, this echo of a distant past (and echoes are seldom more than a bark, no matter how pure-voiced the caller), was it worth the ruin of our home and the grief of my mother?

The duel was fought in a snow-storm on the bank of a frozen brook. Two shots were exchanged before my father fell face downwards on a blue-gray army-cloak spread on the snow. Palchin, his hands trembling, lit a cigarette. Captain Belov hailed the coachmen who were humbly waiting some distance away on the snow-swept road. The whole beastly affair had lasted three minutes.

In *Lost Property* Sebastian gives his own impressions of that lugubrious January day. "Neither my stepmother," he writes, "nor any one of the household knew of the pending affair. On the eve, at dinner, my father threw bread-pellets at me across the table: I had been sulking all day because of some fiendish woollies which the doctor had insisted upon my wearing, and he was trying to cheer me up; but I frowned and blushed and turned away. After dinner we sat in his study, he sipping his coffee and listening to my stepmother's account of the noxious way Mademoiselle had of giving my small half-brother sweets after putting him to bed; and I, at the far end of the room, on the sofa, turning the pages of *Chums*: 'Look out for the next instalment of this rattling yarn.' Jokes at the bottom of the large thin pages. 'The guest of honour had been shown over the School: What struck you most?—A pea from a pea-shooter.' Express-trains roaring through the night. The cricket Blue who fielded the knife thrown by a vicious Malay at the cricketer's friend . . . That 'uproarious' serial featuring three boys, one of whom was a contortionist who could make his nose spin, the second a conjuror, the third a ventriloquist . . . A horseman leaping over a racing-car . . .

"Next morning at school, I made a bad mess of the geometrical problem which in our slang we termed 'Pythagoras' Pants.' The morning was so dark that the lights were turned on in the classroom and this always gave me a nasty buzzing in the head. I came home about half past three in the afternoon with that sticky sense of uncleanliness which I always brought back from school and which was now enhanced by ticklish underclothes. My father's orderly was sobbing in the hall."

THE REAL LIFE OF SEBASTIAN KNIGHT

IN HIS slapdash and very mislead-
ing book, Mr. Goodman paints in a few ill-chosen sentences
a ridiculously wrong picture of Sebastian Knight's childhood. It is one thing to be an author's secretary, it is quite
another to set down an author's life; and if such a task is
prompted by the desire to get one's book into the market
while the flowers on a fresh grave may still be watered with
profit, it is still another matter to try to combine commercial
haste with exhaustive research, fairness and wisdom. I am
not out to damage anybody's reputation. There is no libel
in asserting that alone the impetus of a clicking typewriter
could enable Mr. Goodman to remark that "a Russian education was forced upon a small boy always conscious of the
rich English strain in his blood." This foreign influence, Mr.
Goodman goes on, "brought acute suffering to the child,
so that in his riper years it was with a shudder that he recalled the bearded moujiks, the ikons, the drone of balalaikas,
all of which displaced a healthy English upbringing."

It is hardly worth while pointing out that Mr. Goodman's
concept of Russian surroundings is no truer to nature than,
say, a Kalmuk's notion of England as a dark place where
small boys are flogged to death by red-whiskered school-
masters. What should be really stressed is the fact that
Sebastian was brought up in an atmosphere of intellectual
refinement, blending the spiritual grace of a Russian house-

15

hold with the very best treasures of European culture, and that whatever Sebastian's own reaction to his Russian memories, its complex and special nature never sank to the vulgar level suggested by his biographer.

I remember Sebastian as a boy, six years my senior, gloriously messing about with water-colours in the homely aura of a stately kerosene lamp whose pink silk shade seems painted by his own very wet brush, now that it glows in my memory. I see myself, a child of four or five, on tiptoe, straining and fidgeting, trying to get a better glimpse of the paintbox beyond my half-brother's moving elbow; sticky reds and blues, so well-licked and worn that the enamel gleams in their cavities. There is a slight clatter every time Sebastian mixes his colours on the inside of the tin lid, and the water in the glass before him is clouded with magic hues. His dark hair, closely cropped, renders a small birthmark visible above his rose-red diaphanous ear,—I have clambered onto a chair by now—but he continues to pay no attention to me, until with a precarious lunge, I try to dab the bluest cake in the box, and then, with a shove of his shoulder he pushes me away, still not turning, still as silent and distant, as always in regard to me. I remember peering over the banisters and seeing him come up the stairs, after school, dressed in the black regulation uniform with that leather belt I secretly coveted, mounting slowly, slouchingly, lugging his piebald satchel behind him, patting the banisters and now and then pulling himself up over two or three steps at a time. My lips pursed, I squeeze out a white spittal which falls down and down, always missing Sebastian; and this I do not because I want to annoy him, but merely as a wistful and vain attempt to make him notice my existence. I have a vivid recollection, too, of his riding a bicycle with very low handle-bars along a sun-dappled path in the park of our countryplace, spinning on slowly, the pedals motionless, and I trotting behind, trotting a little faster as his sandled foot presses down the pedal; I am doing my best to keep pace with his tick-tick-sizzling back-wheel, but he heeds me not and soon leaves me hopelessly behind, very out of breath and still trotting.

Then later on, when he was sixteen and I ten, he would sometimes help me with my lessons, explaining things in such a rapid impatient way, that nothing ever came of his assistance and after a while he would pocket his pencil and stalk out of the room. At that period he was tall and sallow-complexioned with a dark shadow above his upper lip. His hair was now glossily parted, and he wrote verse in a black copybook which he kept locked up in his drawer.

I once discovered where he kept the key (in a chink of the wall near the white Dutch stove in his room) and I opened that drawer. There was the copybook; also the photograph of a sister of one of his schoolmates; some gold coins; and a small muslin bag of violet sweets. The poems were written in English. We had had English lessons at home not long before my father's death, and although I never could learn to speak the language fluently, I read and wrote it with comparative ease. I dimly recollect the verse was very romantic, full of dark roses and stars and the call of the sea; but one detail stands out perfectly plain in my memory: the signature under each poem was a little black chess-knight drawn in ink.

I have endeavoured to form a coherent picture of what I saw of my half-brother in those childhood days of mine, between say 1910 (my first year of consciousness) and 1919 (the year he left for England). But the task eludes me. Sebastian's image does not appear as part of my boyhood, thus subject to endless selection and development, nor does it appear as a succession of familiar visions, but it comes to me in a few bright patches, as if he were not a constant member of our family, but some erratic visitor passing across a lighted room and then for a long interval fading into the night. I explain this not so much by the fact that my own childish interests precluded any conscious relation with one who was not young enough to be my companion and not old enough to be my guide, but by Sebastian's constant aloofness, which, although I loved him dearly, never allowed my affection either recognition or food. I could perhaps describe the way he walked, or laughed or sneezed, but all this would be no more than sundry bits of cinema-film cut away by scissors and having nothing in common with the essential drama. And drama there was. Sebastian could never forget his mother, nor could he forget that his father had died for her. That her name was never mentioned in our home added morbid glamour to the remembered charm which suffused his impressionable soul. I do not know whether he could recall with any clarity the time when she was his father's wife; probably he could in a way, as a soft radiance in the background of his life. Nor can I tell what he felt at seeing his mother again when a boy of nine. My mother says he was listless and tongue-tied, afterwards never mentioning that short and pathetically incomplete meeting. In *Lost Property* Sebastian hints at a vaguely bitter feeling towards his happily remarried father, a feeling which changed into one of ecstatic worship when he learnt the reason of his father's fatal duel.

"My discovery of England," writes Sebastian (*Lost Property*), "put new life into my most intimate memories . . . After

Cambridge I took a trip to the Continent and spent a quiet fortnight at Monte Carlo. I think there is some Casino place there, where people gamble, but if so, I missed it, as most of my time was taken up by the composition of my first novel— a very pretentious affair which I am glad to say was turned down by almost as many publishers as my next book had readers. One day I went for a long walk and found a place called Roquebrune. It was at Roquebrune that my mother had died thirteen years before. I well remember the day my father told me of her death and the name of the pension where it occurred. The name was 'Les Violettes.' I asked a chauffeur whether he knew of such a house, but he did not. Then I asked a fruit-seller and he showed me the way. I came at last to a pinkish villa roofed with the typical Provence round red tiles, and I noticed a bunch of violets clumsily painted on the gate. So this was the house. I crossed the garden and spoke to the landlady. She said she had only lately taken over the pension from the former owner and knew nothing of the past. I asked her permission to sit awhile in the garden. An old man naked as far down as I could see peered at me from a balcony, but otherwise there was no one about. I sat down on a blue bench under a great eucalyptus, its bark half stripped away, as seems to be always the case with this sort of tree. Then I tried to see the pink house and the tree and the whole complexion of the place as my mother had seen it. I regretted not knowing the exact window of her room. Judging by the villa's name, I felt sure that there had been before her eyes that same bed of purple pansies. Gradually I worked myself into such a state that for a moment the pink and green seemed to shimmer and float as if seen through a veil of mist. My mother, a dim slight figure in a large hat, went slowly up the steps which seemed to dissolve into water. A terrific thump made me regain consciousness. An orange had rolled down out of the paper bag on my lap. I picked it up and left the garden. Some months later in London I happened to meet a cousin of hers. A turn of the conversation led me to mention that I had visited the place where she had died. 'Oh,' he said, 'but it was the other Roquebrune, the one in the Var.' "

It is curious to note that Mr. Goodman, quoting the same passage, is content to comment that "Sebastian Knight was so enamoured of the burlesque side of things and so incapable of caring for their serious core that he managed, without being by nature either callous or cynical, to make fun of intimate emotions, rightly held sacred by the rest of humanity." No wonder this solemn biographer is out of tune with his hero at every point of the story.

For reasons already mentioned I shall not attempt to describe Sebastian's boyhood with anything like the methodical continuity which I would have normally achieved had Sebastian been a character of fiction. Had it been thus I could have hoped to keep the reader instructed and entertained by picturing my hero's smooth development from infancy to youth. But if I should try this with Sebastian the result would be one of those "biographies romancées" which are by far the worst kind of literature yet invented. So let the door be closed leaving but a thin line of taut light underneath, let that lamp go out too in the neighboring room where Sebastian has gone to bed; let the beautiful olivaceous house on the Neva embankment fade out gradually in the gray-blue frosty night, with gently falling snowflakes lingering in the moon-white blaze of the tall street lamp and powdering the mighty limbs of the two bearded corbel figures which support with an Atlas-like effort the oriel of my father's room. My father is dead, Sebastian is asleep, or at least mouse-quiet, in the next room—and I am lying in bed, wide awake, staring into the darkness.

Some twenty years later, I undertook a journey to Lausanne in order to find the old Swiss lady who had been first Sebastian's governess, then mine. She must have been about fifty when she left us in 1914; correspondence between us had long ceased, so I was not at all sure of finding her still alive, in 1936. But I did. There existed, as I discovered, a union of old Swiss women who had been governesses in Russia before the revolution. They "lived in their past," as the very kind gentleman who guided me there explained, spending their last years—and most of these ladies were decrepit and dotty—comparing notes, having petty feuds with one another and reviling the state of affairs in the Switzerland they had discovered after their many years of life in Russia. Their tragedy lay in the fact that during all those years spent in a foreign country they had kept absolutely immune to its influence (even to the extent of not learning the simplest Russian words); somewhat hostile to their surroundings—how often have I heard Mademoiselle bemoan her exile, complain of being slighted and misunderstood, and yearn for her fair native land; but when these poor wandering souls came home, they found themselves complete strangers in a changed country, so that by a queer trick of sentiment—Russia (which to them had really been an unknown abyss, remotely rumbling beyond a lamplit corner of a stuffy back-room with family photographs in mother-of-pearl frames and a water-colour view of Chillon castle), unknown Russia now took on the aspect of a lost paradise, a vast, vague but retrospectively

21

friendly place, peopled with wistful fancies. I found Mademoiselle very deaf and gray, but as voluble as ever, and after the first effusive embraces she started to recall little facts of my childhood which were either hopelessly distorted, or so foreign to my memory that I doubted their past reality. She knew nothing of my mother's death; nor did she know of Sebastian's having died three months ago. Incidentally, she was also ignorant of his having been a great writer. She was very tearful and her tears were very sincere, but it seemed to annoy her somehow that I did not join in the crying. "You were always so self-controlled," she said. I told her I was writing a book about Sebastian and asked her to talk about his childhood. She had come to our house soon after my father's second marriage, but the past in her mind was so blurred and displaced that she talked of my father's first wife ("cette horrible Anglaise") as if she had known her as well as she had my mother ("cette femme admirable"). "My poor little Sebastian," she wailed, "so tender to me, so noble. Ah, how I remember the way he had of flinging his little arms round my neck and saying: 'I hate everybody except you, Zelle, you alone understand my soul.' And that day when I gently smacked his hand,—une toute petite tape—for being rude to your mother,—the expression of his eyes—it made me want to cry—and his voice when he said: 'I am grateful to you, Zelle. It shall never happen again . . .' "

She went on in this fashion for quite a long time, making me dismally uncomfortable. I managed at last, after several fruitless attempts, to turn the conversation—I was quite hoarse by that time as she had mislaid her ear-trumpet. Then she spoke of her neighbour, a fat little creature still older than she, whom I had met in the passage. "The good woman is quite deaf," she complained, "and a dreadful liar. I know for certain that she only gave lessons to the Princess Demidov's children—never lived there." "Write that book, that beautiful book," she cried as I was leaving, "make it a fairy-tale with Sebastian for prince. The enchanted prince . . . Many a time have I said to him: Sebastian, be careful, women will adore you. And he would reply with a laugh: Well, I'll adore women too . . ."

I squirmed inwardly. She gave me a smacking kiss and patted my hand and was tearful again. I glanced at her misty old eyes, at the dead lustre of her false teeth, at the well-remembered garnet brooch on her bosom . . . We parted. It was raining hard and I felt ashamed and cross at having interrupted my second chapter to make this useless pilgrimage. One impression especially upset me. She had not asked one single thing about Sebastian's later life, not a single question about the way he had died, nothing.

IN NOVEMBER of 1918 my mother
resolved to flee with Sebastian and myself from the dangers
of Russia. Revolution was in full swing, frontiers were closed.
She got in touch with a man who had made smuggling
refugees across the border his profession, and it was settled
that for a certain fee, one half of which was paid in advance,
he would get us to Finland. We were to leave the train just
before the frontier, at a place we could lawfully reach, and
then cross over by secret paths, doubly, trebly secret owing
to the heavy snowfalls in that silent region. At the starting-
point of our train journey, we found ourselves, my mother
and I, waiting for Sebastian, who, with the heroic help of
Captain Belov, was trundling the luggage from house to station. The train was scheduled to start at 8:40 A. M. Half
past and still no Sebastian. Our guide was already in the train
and sat quietly reading a newspaper; he had warned my
mother that in no circumstance should she talk to him in
public, and as the time passed and the train was preparing to
leave, a nightmare feeling of numb panic began to come over
us. We knew that the man in accordance with the traditions
of his profession, would never renew a performance that had
misfired at the outset. We knew too that we could not again
afford the expenses of flight. The minutes passed and I felt
something gurgling desperately in the pit of my stomach. The
thought that in a minute or two the train would move off and

that we should have to return to a dark cold attic (our house had been nationalised some months ago) was utterly disastrous. On our way to the station we had passed Sebastian and Belov pushing the heavily burdened wheelbarrow through the crunching snow. This picture now stood motionless before my eyes (I was a boy of thirteen and very imaginative) as a charmed thing doomed to its paralysed eternity. My mother, her hands in her sleeves and a wisp of grey hair emerging from beneath her woolen kerchief, walked to and fro, trying to catch the eye of our guide every time she passed by his window. Eight forty-five, eight-fifty . . . The train was late in starting, but at last the whistle blew, a rush of warm white smoke raced its shadow across the brown snow on the platform, and at the same time Sebastian appeared running, the earflaps of his fur cap flying in the wind. The three of us scrambled into the moving train. It took some time before he managed to tell us that Captain Belov had been arrested in the street just as they were passing the house where he had lived before, and that leaving the luggage to its fate, he, Sebastian, had made a desperate dash for the station. A few months later we learned that our poor friend had been shot, together with a score of people in the same batch, shoulder to shoulder with Palchin, who died as bravely as Belov.

In his last published book, *The Doubtful Asphodel* (1936), Sebastian depicts an episodical character who has just escaped from an unnamed country of terror and misery. "What can I tell you of my past, gentlemen [he is saying], I was born in a land where the idea of freedom, the notion of right, the habit of human kindness were things coldly despised and brutally outlawed. Now and then, in the course of history, a hypocrite government would paint the walls of the nation's prison a comelier shade of yellow and loudly proclaim the granting of rights familiar to happier states; but either these rights were solely enjoyed by the jailers or else they contained some secret flaw which made them even more bitter than the decrees of frank tyranny ... Every man in the land was a slave, if he was not a bully; since the soul and everything pertaining to it were denied to man, the infliction of physical pain came to be considered as sufficient to govern and guide human nature ... From time to time a thing called revolution would occur, turning the slaves into bullies and vice versa ... A dark country, a hellish place, gentlemen, and if there is anything of which I am certain in life it is that I shall never exchange the liberty of my exile for the vile parody of home ..."

Owing to there being in this character's speech a chance reference to "great woods and snow-covered plains," Mr. Goodman promptly assumes that the whole passage tallies with Sebastian Knight's own attitude to Russia. This is a grotesque misconception; it should be quite clear to any unbiased reader that the quoted words refer rather to a fanciful amalgamation of tyrannic iniquities than to any particular nation or historical reality. And if I attach them to that part of my story which deals with Sebastian's escape from revolutionary Russia it is because I want to follow it up immediately with a few sentences borrowed from his most autobiographical work: "I always think," he writes (*Lost Property*), "that one of the purest emotions is that of the banished man pining after the land of his birth. I would have liked to show him straining his memory to the utmost in a continuous effort to keep alive and bright the vision of his past: the blue remembered hills and the happy highways, the hedge with its unofficial rose and the field with its rabbits, the distant spire and the near bluebell . . . But because the theme has already been treated by my betters and also because I have an innate distrust of what I feel easy to express, no sentimental wanderer will ever be allowed to land on the rock of my unfriendly prose."

Whatever the particular conclusion of this passage, it is obvious that only one who has known what it is to leave a dear country could thus be tempted by the picture of nostalgia. I find it impossible to believe that Sebastian, no matter how gruesome the aspect of Russia was at the time of our escape, did not feel the wrench we all experienced. All things considered, it had been his home, and the set of kindly, well-meaning, gentle-mannered people driven to death or exile for the sole crime of their existing, was the set to which he too belonged. His dark youthful broodings, the romantic—and let me add, somewhat artificial—passion for his mother's land, could not, I am sure, exclude real affection for the country where he had been born and bred.

After having tumbled silently into Finland, we lived for a time in Helsingfors. Then our ways parted. My mother acting on the suggestion of an old friend took me to Paris, where I continued my education. And Sebastian went to London and Cambridge. His mother had left him a comfortable income and whatever worries assailed him in later life, they were never monetary. Just before he left, we sat down, the three of us, for the minute of silence according to Russian tradition. I remember the way my mother sat, with her hands in her lap twirling my father's wedding-ring (as she usually did when inactive) which she wore on the same finger as her own and which was so large that she had tied it to her own with black thread. I remember Sebastian's pose too; he was dressed in a dark-blue suit and he sat with his legs crossed, the upper foot gently swinging. I stood up first, then he, then my mother. He had made us promise not to see him to the boat, so it was there, in that whitewashed room, that we said good-bye. My mother made a quick little sign of the cross over his inclined face and a moment later we saw him through the window, getting into the taxi with his bag, in the last hunch-backed attitude of the departing.

We did not hear from him very often, nor were his letters very long. During his three years at Cambridge, he visited us in Paris but twice,—better say once, for the second time was when he came over for my mother's funeral. She and I talked of him fairly frequently, especially in the last years of her life, when she was quite aware of her approaching end. It was she who told me of Sebastian's strange adventure in 1917 of which I then knew nothing, as at the time I had happened to be on a holiday in the Crimea. It appears that Sebastian had developed a friendship with the futurist poet Alexis Pan and his wife Larissa, a weird couple who rented a cottage close to our country estate near Luga. He was a noisy robust little man with a gleam of real talent concealed in the messy obscurity of his verse. But because he did his best to shock people with his monstrous mass of otiose words (he was the inventor of the "submental grunt" as he called it), his main output seems now so nugatory, so false, so old-fashioned (super-modern things have a queer knack of dating much faster than others) that his true value is only remembered by a few scholars who admire the magnificent translations of English poems made by him at the very outset of his literary career,—one of these at least being a very miracle of verbal transfusion: his Russian rendering of Keats's "La Belle Dame Sans Merci."

So one morning in early summer seventeen-year-old Sebastian disappeared, leaving my mother a short note which informed her that he was accompanying Pan and his wife on a journey to the East. At first she took it to be a joke (Sebastian, for all his moodiness, at times devised some piece of ghoulish fun, as when in a crowded tramcar he had the ticket-collector transmit to a girl in the far end of the car a scribbled message which really ran thus: I am only a poor ticket-collector, but I love you); when, however, she called upon the Pans she actually found that they had left. It transpired somewhat later that Pan's idea of a Marcopolian journey consisted in gently working eastwards from one provincial town to another, arranging in every one a "lyrical surprise," that is, renting a hall (or a shed if no hall was available) and holding there a poetical performance whose net profit was supposed to get him, his wife and Sebastian to the next town. It was never made clear in what Sebastian's functions, help or duties lay, or if he was merely supposed to hover around, to fetch things when needed and to be nice to Larissa, who had a quick temper and was not easily soothed. Alexis Pan generally appeared on the stage dressed in a morning coat, perfectly correct but for its being embroidered with huge lotus flowers. A constellation (the Greater Dog) was painted on his bald brow. He delivered his verse in a great booming voice which, coming from so small a man, made one think of a mouse engendering mountains. Next to him on the platform sat Larissa, a large equine woman in a mauve dress, sewing on buttons or patching up a pair of old trousers, the point being that she never did any of these things for her husband in everyday life. Now and then, between two poems, Pan would perform a slow dance—a mixture of Javanese wrist-play and his own rhythmic inventions. After recitals he got gloriously soused—and this was his undoing. The journey to the East ended in Simbirsk with Alexis dead-drunk and penniless in a filthy inn and Larissa and her tantrums locked up at the police-station for having slapped the face of some meddlesome official who had disapproved of her husband's noisy genius. Sebastian came home as nonchalantly as he had left. "Any other boy," added my mother, "would have looked rather sheepish and rightly ashamed of the whole foolish affair," but Sebastian talked of his trip as of some quaint incident of which he had been a dispassionate observer. Why he had joined in that ludicrous show and what in fact had led him to pal with that grotesque couple remained a complete mystery (my mother thought that perhaps he had been ensnared by Larissa but the woman was perfectly plain, elderly and violently in love with her freak of a husband). They dropped out of Sebastian's life soon after. Two or three years later Pan enjoyed a short artificial vogue in Bolshevik surroundings which was due I think to the queer notion (mainly based on a muddle of terms) that there is a natural connection between extreme politics and extreme art. Then, in 1922 or 1923 Alexis Pan committed suicide with the aid of a pair of braces.

"I've always felt," said my mother, "that I never really knew Sebastian, I knew he obtained good marks at school, read an astonishing number of books, was clean in his habits, insisted on taking a cold bath every morning although his lungs were none too strong,—I knew all this and more, but he himself escaped me. And now that he lives in a strange country and writes to us in English I cannot help thinking that he will always remain an enigma,—though the Lord knows how hard I have tried to be kind to the boy."

When Sebastian visited us in Paris at the close of his first university year, I was struck by his foreign appearance. He wore a canary yellow jumper under his tweed coat. His flannel trousers were baggy, and his thick socks sagged, innocent of suspenders. The stripes of his tie were loud and for some odd reason he carried his handkerchief in his sleeve. He smoked his pipe in the street, knocking it out against his heel. He had developed a new way of standing with his back to the fire, his hands deep in his trouser pockets. He spoke Russian gingerly, lapsing into English as soon as the conversation drew out to anything longer than a couple of sentences. He stayed exactly one week.

The next time he came, my mother was no more. We sat together for a long time after the funeral. He awkwardly patted me on the shoulder when the chance sight of her spectacles lying alone on a shelf sent me into shivers of tears which I had managed to restrain until then. He was very kind and helpful in a distant vague way, as if he was thinking of something else all the time. We discussed matters and he suggested my coming to the Riviera and then to England; I had just finished my schooling. I said I preferred pottering on in Paris where I had a number of friends. He did not insist. The question of money was also touched on and he remarked in his queer off-hand way that he could always let me have as much cash as I might require,—I think he used the word "tin," though I am not sure. Next day he left for the South of France. In the morning we went for a short stroll and as it usually happened when we were alone together I was curiously embarrassed, every now and then catching myself painfully digging for a topic of conversation. He was silent too. Just before parting he said: "Well, that's that. If you need anything write me to my London address. I hope your Sore-bone works out as well as my Cambridge. And by the way try and find some subject you like and stick to it—until you find it bores you." There was a slight twinkle in his dark eyes. "Good luck," he said, "cheerio,"—and shook my hand in the limp self-conscious fashion he had acquired in England. Suddenly for no earthly reason I felt immensely sorry for him and longed to say something real, something with wings and a heart, but the birds I wanted settled on my shoulders and head only later when I was alone and not in need of words.

THE REAL LIFE OF SEBASTIAN KNIGHT

TWO months had elapsed after Sebastian's death when this book was started. Well do I know how much he would have hated my waxing sentimental, but still I cannot help saying that my life-long affection for him, which somehow or other had always been crushed and thwarted, now leapt into new being with such a blaze of emotional strength—that all my other affairs were turned into flickering silhouettes. During our rare meetings we had never discussed literature, and now when the possibility of any sort of communication between us was barred by the strange habit of human death, I regretted desperately never having told Sebastian how much I delighted in his books. As it is I find myself helplessly wondering whether he had been aware I had ever read them.

But what actually did I know about Sebastian? I might devote a couple of chapters to the little I remembered of his childhood and youth—but what next? As I planned my book it became evident that I would have to undertake an immense amount of research, bringing up his life bit by bit and soldering the fragments with my inner knowledge of his character. Inner knowledge? Yes, this was a thing I possessed, I felt it in every nerve. And the more I pondered on it, the more I perceived that I had yet another tool in my hand: when I imagined actions of his which I heard of only after his death, I knew for certain that in such or such a case I should have acted just as he had. Once I happened to see two brothers, tennis champions, matched against one another; their strokes were totally different, and one of the two was far, far better than the other; but the general rhythm of their motions as they swept all over the court was exactly the same, so that had it been possible to draft both systems two identical designs would have appeared.

I daresay Sebastian and I also had some kind of common rhythm; this might explain the curious "it-has-happened-before-feeling" which seizes me when following the bends of his life. And if, as often was the case with him, the "why's" of his behaviour were as many X's, I often find their meaning disclosed now in a subconscious turn of this or that sentence put down by me. This is not meant to imply that I shared with him any riches of the mind, any facets of talent. Far from it. His genius always seemed to me a miracle utterly independent of any of the definite things we may have both experienced in the similar background of our childhood. I may have seen and remembered what he saw and remembered, but the difference between his power of expression and mine is comparable to that which exists between a Bechstein piano and a baby's rattle. I would never have let him see the least sentence of this book lest he should wince at the way I manage my miserable English. And wince he would. Nor do I dare imagine his reactions had he learnt that before starting on his biography, his half-brother (whose literary experience had amounted till then to one or two chance English translations required by a motor-firm) had decided to take up a "be-an-author" course buoyantly advertised in an English magazine. Yes, I confess to it,—not that I regret it. The gentleman, who for a reasonable fee was supposed to make a successful writer of my person,—really took the utmost pains to teach me to be coy and graceful, forcible and crisp, and if I proved a hopeless pupil—although he was far too kind to admit it,—it was because from the very start I had been hypnotised by the perfect glory of a short story which he sent me as a sample of what his pupils could do and sell. It contained among other things a wicked Chinaman who snarled, a brave girl with hazel eyes and a big quiet fellow whose knuckles turned white when someone really annoyed him. I would now refrain from mentioning this rather eerie business did it not disclose how unprepared I was for my task and to what wild extremities my diffidence drove me. When at last I did take pen in hand, I had composèd myself to face the inevitable which is but another way of saying I was ready to try and do my best.

There is still another little moral lurking behind this affair. If Sebastian had followed the same kind of correspondence course just for the fun of the thing, just to see what would have happened (he appreciated such amusements), he would have turned out an incalculably more hopeless pupil than I. Told to write like Mr. Everyman he would have written like none. I cannot even copy his manner because the manner of his prose was the manner of his thinking and that was a dazzling succession of gaps; and you cannot ape a gap because you are bound to fill it in somehow or other—and blot it out in the process. But when in Sebastian's books I find some detail of mood or impression which makes me remember at once, say, a certain effect of lighting in a definite place which we two had noticed, unknown to one another, then I feel that in spite of the toe of his talent being beyond my reach we did possess certain psychological affinities which will help me out.

The tool was there, it must now be put to use. My first duty after Sebastian's death was to go through his belongings. He had left everything to me and I had a letter from him instructing me to burn certain of his papers. It was so obscurely worded that at first I thought it might refer to rough drafts or discarded manuscripts, but I soon found out that except for a few odd pages dispersed among other papers, he himself had destroyed them long ago, for he belonged to that rare type of writer who knows that nothing ought to remain except the perfect achievement: the printed book; that its actual existence is inconsistent with that of its spectre, the uncouth manuscript flaunting its imperfections like a revengeful ghost carrying its own head under its arm; and that for this reason the litter of the workshop, no matter its sentimental or commercial value, must never subsist.

When for the first time in my life I visited Sebastian's small flat in London at 36 Oak Park Gardens, I had an empty feeling of having postponed an appointment until too late. Three rooms, a cold fireplace, silence. During the last years of his life he had not lived there very much, nor had he died there. Half a dozen suits, mostly old, were hanging in the wardrobe, and for a second I had an odd impression of Sebastian's body being stiffly multiplied in a succession of square-shouldered forms. I had seen him once in that brown coat; I touched its sleeve, but it was limp and irresponsive to that faint call of memory. There were shoes too, which had walked many miles and had now reached the end of their journey. Folded shirts lying on their backs. What could all these quiet things tell me of Sebastian? His bed. A small old oil-painting, a little cracked (muddy road, rainbow, beautiful puddles) on the ivory white of the wall above. The eye-spot of his awakening.

As I looked about me, all things in that bedroom seemed to have just jumped back in the nick of time as if caught unawares, and now were gradually returning my gaze, trying to see whether I had noticed their guilty start. This was particularly the case with the low, white-robed arm-chair near the bed; I wondered what it had stolen. Then by groping in the recesses of its reluctant folds I found something hard: it turned out to be a Brazil nut, and the armchair again folding its arms resumed its inscrutable expression (which might have been one of contemptuous dignity).

The bathroom. The glass shelf, bare save for an empty talc-powder tin with violets figured between its shoulders, standing there alone, reflected in the mirror like a coloured advertisement.

Then I examined the two main rooms. The dining-room was curiously impersonal, like all places where people eat,—perhaps because food is our chief link with the common chaos of matter rolling about us. There was, it is true, a cigarette end in a glass ashtray, but it had been left there by a certain Mr. McMath, house-agent.

The study. From here one got a view of the back-garden or park, the fading sky, a couple of elms, not oaks, in spite of the street-name's promise. A leather divan sprawling at one end of the room. Bookshelves densely peopled. The writing-desk. There was almost nothing on it: a red pencil, a box of paper clips—it looked sullen and distant, but the lamp on its western edge was adorable. I found its pulse and the opal globe melted into light: that magic moon had seen Sebastian's white moving hand. Now I was really getting down to business. I took the key that had been bequeathed me and unlocked the drawers.

First of all I dislodged the two bundles of letters on which Sebastian had scribbled: to be destroyed. One was folded in such a fashion that I could not get a glimpse of the writing: the note-paper was egg-shell blue with a dark-blue rim. The other packet consisted of a medley of note-paper crisscrossed in a bold feminine scrawl. I guessed whose it was. For a wild instant I struggled with the temptation to examine closer both bundles. I am sorry to say the better man won. But as I was burning them in the grate one sheet of the blue became loose, curving backwards under the torturing flame, and before the crumpling blackness had crept over it, a few words appeared in full radiance, then swooned and all was over.

I sank down in an armchair and mused for some moments. The words I had seen were Russian words, part of a Russian sentence,—quite insignificant in themselves, really (not that I might have expected from the flame of chance the slick intent of a novelist's plot). The literal English translation would be "thy manner always to find" . . . —and it was not the sense that struck me, but the mere fact of its being in my language. I had not the vaguest inkling as to who she might be, that Russian woman whose letters Sebastian had kept in close proximity to those of Clare Bishop—and somehow it perplexed and bothered me. From my chair beside the fireplace, which was again black and cold, I could see the fair light of the lamp on the desk, the bright whiteness of paper brimming over the open drawer and one sheet of foolscap lying alone on the blue carpet, half in shade, cut diagonally by the limit of the light. For a moment I seemed to see a transparent Sebastian at his desk; or rather I thought of that passage about the wrong Roquebrune: perhaps he preferred doing his writing in bed?

After a while I went on with my business, examining and roughly classifying the contents of the drawers. There were many letters. These I set aside to be gone through later. Newspaper cuttings in a gaudy book, an impossible butterfly on its cover. No, none of them were reviews of his own books: Sebastian was much too vain to collect them; nor would his sense of humour allow him to paste them in patiently when they did come his way. Still, as I say, there was an album with cuttings, all of them referring (as I found out later when perusing them at leisure) to incongruous or dream-absurd incidents which had occurred in the most trivial places and conditions. Mixed metaphors too, I perceived, met with his approval, as he probably considered them to belong to the same faintly nightmare category. Between some legal documents I found a slip of paper on which he had begun to write a story—there was only one sentence, stopping short but it gave me the opportunity of observing the queer way Sebastian had—in the process of writing—of not striking out the words which he had replaced by others, so that, for instance, the phrase I encountered ran thus: "As he a heavy A heavy sleeper, Roger Rogerson, old Rogerson bought old Rogers bought, so afraid Being a heavy sleeper, old Rogers was so afraid of missing to-morrows. He was a heavy sleeper. He was mortally afraid of missing to-morrow's event glory early train glory so what he did was to buy and bring home in a to buy that evening and bring home not one but eight alarm clocks of different sizes and vigour of ticking nine eight eleven alarm clocks of different sizes ticking which alarm clocks nine alarm clocks as a cat has nine which he placed which made his bedroom look rather like a"

I was sorry it stopped here.

Foreign coins in a chocolate box: francs, marks, schillings, crowns,—and their small change. Several fountain pens. An Oriental amethyst, unset. A rubber band. A glass tube of tablets for headache, nervous breakdown, neuralgia, insomnia, bad dreams, toothache. The toothache sounded rather dubious. An old note-book (1926) filled with dead telephone numbers. Photographs.

I thought I should find lots of girls. You know the kind,—smiling in the sun, summer snapshots, continental tricks of shade, smiling in white on pavement, sand or snow,—but I was mistaken. The two dozen or so of photographs I shook out of a large envelope with the laconic Mr. H. written on top in Sebastian's hand, all featured one and the same person at different stages of his life: first a moonfaced urchin in a vulgarly cut sailor suit, next an ugly boy in a cricket-cap, then a pug-nosed youth and so on till one arrived at a series of full-grown Mr. H.—a rather repellent bulldog type of man, getting steadily fatter in a world of photographic backgrounds and real front gardens. I learnt who the man was supposed to be when I came across a newspaper clipping attached to one of the photographs:

"Author writing fictitious biography requires photos of gentleman, efficient appearance, plain, steady, teetotaller, bachelors preferred. Will pay for photos childhood, youth, manhood to appear in said work."

That was a book Sebastian never wrote, but possibly he was still contemplating doing so in the last year of his life, for the last photograph of Mr. H. standing happily near a brand-new car, bore the date "March 1935" and Sebastian had died but a year later.

Suddenly I felt tired and miserable. I wanted the face of his Russian correspondent. I wanted pictures of Sebastian himself. I wanted many things ... Then, as I let my eyes roam around the room, I caught sight of a couple of framed photographs in the dim shadows above the bookshelves.

I got up and examined them. One was an enlarged snapshot of a Chinese stripped to the waist, in the act of being vigourously beheaded, the other was a banal photographic study of a curly child playing with a pup. The taste of their juxtaposition seemed to me questionable, but probably Sebastian had his own reasons for keeping and hanging them so.

I glanced too, at the books; they were numerous, untidy and miscellaneous. But one shelf was a little neater than the rest and here I noted the following sequence which for a moment seemed to form a vague musical phrase, oddly familiar: *Hamlet*, *La morte d'Arthur*, *The Bridge of San Luis Rey*, *Doctor Jekyll and Mr. Hyde*, *South Wind*, *The Lady with the Dog*, *Madame Bovary*, *The Invisible Man*, *Le Temps Retrouvé*, *Anglo-Persian Dictionary*, *The Author of Trixie*, *Alice in Wonderland*, *Ulysses*, *About Buying a Horse*, *King Lear* ...

The melody gave a small gasp and faded. I returned to the desk and began sorting out the letters I had laid aside. They were mostly business letters, and I felt entitled to peruse them. Some bore no relation to Sebastian's profession, others did. The disorder was considerable and many allusions remained unintelligible to me. In a few cases he had kept copies of his own letters so that for instance I got in full a long zestful dialogue between him and his publisher in regard to a certain book. Then, there was a fussy soul in Rumania of all places, clamouring for an option . . . I learnt too of the sales in England and the Dominions . . . Nothing very brilliant—but in one case at least perfectly satisfactory. A few letters from friendly authors. One gentle writer, the author of a single famous book, rebuked Sebastian (April 4, 1928) for being "Conradish" and suggested his leaving out the "con" and cultivating the "radish" in future works—a singularly silly idea, I thought.

Lastly, at the very bottom of the bundle, I came to my mother's and my own letters, together with several from one of his undergraduate friends; and as I struggled a little with their pages (old letters resent being unfolded) I suddenly realised what my next hunting-ground ought to be.

THE REAL LIFE OF
SEBASTIAN KNIGHT

SEBASTIAN KNIGHT'S college
years were not particularly happy. To be sure he enjoyed
many of the things he found at Cambridge,—he was in fact
quite overcome at first to see and smell and feel the country
for which he had always longed. A real hansom-cab took him
from the station to Trinity College: the vehicle, it seemed, had
been waiting there especially for him, desperately holding out
against extinction till that moment, and then gladly dying
out to join side whiskers and the Large Copper. The slush of
streets gleaming wet in the misty darkness with its promised
counterpoint—a cup of strong tea and a generous fire—
formed a harmony which somehow he knew by heart. The
pure chimes of tower-clocks, now hanging over the town,
now overlapping and echoing afar, in some odd, deeply familiar way blended with the piping cries of the newspaper
vendors. And as he entered the stately gloom of Great Court
with gowned shadows passing in the mist and the porter's
bowler hat bobbing in front of him, Sebastian felt that he
somehow recognised every sensation, the wholesome reek of
damp turf, the ancient sonority of stone slabs under heel, the
blurred outlines of dark walls overhead—everything. That
special feeling of elation probably endured for quite a long
time, but there was something else intermingled with it, and
later on predominant. Sebastian in spite of himself realised
with perhaps a kind of helpless amazement (for he had ex-

pected more from England than she could do for him) that no matter how wisely and sweetly his new surroundings played up to his old dreams, he himself, or rather still the most precious part of himself, would remain as hopelessly alone as it had always been. The keynote of Sebastian's life was solitude and the kindlier fate tried to make him feel at home by counterfeiting admirably the things he thought he wanted, the more he was aware of his inability to fit into the picture,—into any kind of picture. When at last he thoroughly understood this and grimly started to cultivate self-consciousness as if it had been some rare talent or passion, only then did Sebastian derive satisfaction from its rich and monstrous growth, ceasing to worry about his awkward uncongeniality,—but that was much later.

Apparently, at first he was frantically afraid of not doing the right thing or, worse still, of doing it clumsily. Someone told him that the hard cornered part of the academical cap ought to be broken, or even removed altogether, leaving only the limp black cloth. No sooner had he done so, than he found out that he had lapsed into the worst "undergrad" vulgarity and that perfect taste consisted in ignoring the cap and gown one wore, thus granting them the faultless appearance of insignificant things which otherwise would have dared to matter. Again, whatever the weather, hats and umbrellas were tabooed, and Sebastian piously got wet and caught colds until a certain day when he came to know one D. W. Gorget, a delightful, flippant, lazy, easy-going fellow, famed for his rowdiness, elegance and wit: and Gorget coolly went about in a town-hat plus umbrella. Fifteen years later, when I visited Cambridge and was told by Sebastian's best college friend (now a prominent scholar) of all these things, I remarked that everybody seemed to be carrying—— "Exactly," said he, "Gorget's umbrella has bred."

"And tell me," I asked, "what about games? Was Sebastian good at games?"

My informant smiled.

"I am afraid," he answered, "that except a little mild tennis on a rather soggy green court with a daisy or two on the worst patches, neither Sebastian nor I went in very much for that sort of thing. His racket, I remember, was a remarkably expensive one, and his flannels very becoming—and generally he looked very tidy and nice and all that; but his service was a feminine pat and he rushed about a lot without hitting anything, and as I was not much better than he, our game mainly consisted in retrieving damp green balls or throwing them back to players on the adjacent courts—all this under a steady drizzle. Yes, he was definitely poor at games."

"Did that upset him?"

"It did in a way. In fact, his first term was quite poisoned by the thought of his inferiority in those matters. The first time he met Gorget,—that was in my rooms—poor Sebastian talked so much about tennis that at last Gorget asked whether the game was played with a stick. This rather soothed Sebastian as he supposed that Gorget, whom he liked from the start, was bad at games, too."

"And was he?"

"Oh, well, he was a Rugby Blue, but perhaps he did not much care for lawn-tennis. Anyway, Sebastian soon got over the game complex. And generally speaking—"

We sat there in that dimly lit oak-panelled room, our armchairs so low that it was quite easy to reach the tea things which stood humbly on the carpet, and Sebastian's spirit seemed to hover about us with the flicker of the fire reflected in the brass knobs of the hearth. My interlocutor had known him so intimately that I think he was right in suggesting that Sebastian's sense of inferiority was based on his trying to out-England England, and never succeeding, and going on trying, until finally he realised that it was not these outward things that betrayed him, not the mannerisms of fashionable slang, but the very fact of his striving to be and act like other people when he was blissfully condemned to the solitary confinement of his own self.

Still, he had done his best to be a standard undergraduate. Clad in a brown dressing-gown and old pumps, carrying soap-box and sponge-bag, he had strolled out on winter mornings on his way to the Baths round the corner. He had had breakfast in Hall, with the porridge as grey and dull as the sky above Great Court and the orange marmalade of exactly the same hue as the creeper on its walls. He had mounted his "pushbike," as my informant called it, and with his gown across his shoulder had pedalled to this or that lecture hall. He had lunched at the Pitt (which, I understood, was a kind of club, probably with horsey pictures on the walls and very old waiters asking their eternal riddle: thick or clear?). He had played fives (whatever that may be) or some other tame game, and then had had tea with two or three friends; the talk had hobbled along between crumpet and pipe, carefully avoiding anything that had not been said by others. There may have been another lecture or two before dinner, and then again Hall, a very fine place which I was duly shown. It was being swept at the moment, and the fat white calves of Henry the Eighth looked as if they might get tickled.

"And where did Sebastian sit?"

"Down there, against the wall."

"But how did one get there? The tables seem miles long."

"He used to step up on the outer bench and walk across the table. One trod on a plate now and then, but it was the usual method."

Then, after dinner, he would go back to his rooms, or perhaps make his way with some silent companion to the little cinema on the market place where a Wild West film would be shown, or Charlie Chaplin stiffly trotting away from the big wicked man and skidding on the street corner.

Then, after three or four terms of this sort of thing a curious change came over Sebastian. He stopped enjoying what he thought he ought to enjoy and serenely turned to what really concerned him. Outwardly, this change resulted in his dropping out of the rhythm of college life. He saw no one, except my informant, who remained perhaps the only man in his life with whom he had been perfectly frank and natural—it was a handsome friendship and I quite understood Sebastian, for that quiet scholar struck me as being the finest and gentlest soul imaginable. They were both interested in English literature, and Sebastian's friend was already then planning that first work of his, *The Laws of Literary Imagination*, which, two or three years later, won for him the Montgomery Prize.

"I must confess," said he as he stroked a soft blue cat with celadon eyes which had appeared from nowhere and now made itself comfortable in his lap, "I must confess that Sebastian rather pained me at that particular period of our friendship. Missing him in the lecture hall, I would go to his rooms and find him still in bed, curled up like a sleeping child, but gloomily smoking, with cigarette ash all over his crumpled pillow and inkstains on the sheet which hung loosely to the floor. He would only grunt in reply to my energetic greeting, not deigning even to change his position, so after hovering around and satisfying myself that he was not ill, I would go off to lunch, and then call upon him again only to find him lying on his other side and using a slipper for an ashtray. I would suggest getting him something to eat, for his cupboard was always empty, and presently, when I brought him a bunch of bananas, he would cheer up like a monkey and immediately start to annoy me with a series of obscurely immoral statements, related to Life, Death or God, which he specially relished making because he knew that they annoyed me—although I never believed that he really meant what he said.

"At last, about three or four in the afternoon, he would put on his dressing-gown and shuffle into the sitting-room where, in disgust, I would leave him, huddled up by the fire and scratching his head. And next day, as I sat working in my digs, I would suddenly hear a great stamping up the stairs, and Sebastian would bounce into the room, clean, fresh and excited, with the poem he had just finished."

All this, I trust, is very true to type, and one little detail strikes me as especially pathetic. It appears that Sebastian's English, though fluent and idiomatic, was decidedly that of a foreigner. His "r"s, when beginning a word, rolled and rasped, he made queer mistakes, saying, for instance, "I have seized a cold" or "that fellow is sympathetic"—merely meaning that he was a nice chap. He misplaced the accent in such words as "interesting" or "laboratory." He mispronounced names like "Socrates" or "Desdemona." Once corrected, he would never repeat the mistake, but the very fact of his not being quite sure about certain words distressed him enormously and he used to blush a bright pink when, owing to a chance verbal flaw, some utterance of his would not be quite understood by an obtuse listener. In those days, he wrote far better than he spoke, but still there was something vaguely un-English about his poems. None of them have reached me. True, his friend thought that perhaps one or two . . .

He put down the cat and rummaged awhile among some papers in a drawer, but he could not lay his hand on anything. "Perhaps, in some trunk at my sister's place," he said vaguely, "but I'm not even sure . . . Little things like that are the darlings of oblivion, and moreover I know Sebastian would have applauded their loss."

"By the way," I said, "the past you recall seems dismally wet meteorologically speaking,—as dismal, in fact, as today's weather (it was a bleak day in February). Tell me, was it never warm and sunny? Does not Sebastian himself refer somewhere to the 'pink candlesticks of great chestnut trees' along the bank of some beautiful little river?"

Yes, I was right, spring and summer did happen in Cambridge almost every year (that mysterious "almost" was singularly pleasing). Yes, Sebastian quite liked to loll in a punt on the Cam. But what he liked above all was to cycle in the dusk along a certain path skirting meadows. There, he would sit on a fence looking at the wispy salmon-pink clouds turning to a dull copper in the pale evening sky and think about things. What things? That cockney girl with her soft hair still in plaits whom he once followed across the common, and accosted and kissed, and never saw again? The form of a particular cloud? Some misty sunset beyond a black Russian fir-wood (oh, how much I would give for such a memory coming to him!)? The inner meaning of grassblade and star? the unknown language of silence? the terrific weight of a dew-drop? the heartbreaking beauty of a pebble among millions and millions of pebbles, all making sense, but what sense? The old, old question of Who are you? to one's own self grown strangely evasive in the gloaming, and to God's world around to which one has never been really introduced. Or, perhaps, we shall be nearer the truth in supposing that while Sebastian sat on that fence, his mind was a turmoil of words and fancies, uncomplete fancies and insufficient words, but already he knew that this and only this was the reality of his life, and that his destiny lay beyond that ghostly battlefield which he would cross in due time.

"Did I like his books? Oh, enormously. I didn't see much of him after he left Cambridge, and he never sent me any of his works. Authors, you know, are forgetful. But one day I got three of them at the library and read them in as many nights. I was always sure he would produce something fine, but I never expected it would be as fine as that. In his last year here—I don't know what's the matter with this cat, she does not seem to know milk all of a sudden."

In his last Cambridge year Sebastian worked a good deal; his subject—English literature—was a vast and complicated one; but this same period was marked by his sudden trips to London, generally without the authorities' leave. His tutor, the late Mr. Jefferson, had been, I learnt, a mighty dull old gentleman, but a fine linguist, who insisted upon considering Sebastian as a Russian. In other words, he drove Sebastian to the limit of exasperation by telling him all the Russian words he knew,—a nice bagful collected on a journey to Moscow years ago,—and asking him to teach him some more. One day, at last, Sebastian blurted out that there was some mistake—he had not been born in Russia really, but in Sofia. Upon which, the delighted old man at once started to speak Bulgarian. Sebastian lamely answered that it was not the special dialect he knew, and when challenged to furnish a sample, invented a new idiom on the spur of the moment, which greatly puzzled the old linguist until it dawned upon him that Sebastian—

"Well, I think you have drained me now," said my informant with a smile. "My reminiscences are getting shallower and sillier—and I hardly think it worth while to add that Sebastian got a first and that we had our picture taken in full glory—I shall try and find it some day and send it to you if you like. Must you really leave now? Would you not like to see the Backs? Come along and visit the crocuses, Sebastian used to call them 'the poet's mushrooms,' if you see what he meant."

But it was raining too hard. We stood for a minute or two under the porch, and then I said I thought I'd better be going.

"Oh, look here," called Sebastian's friend after me, as I was already picking my way among the puddles. "I quite forgot to tell you. The Master told me the other day that somebody wrote to him asking whether Sebastian Knight had really been a Trinity man. Now, what was the fellow's name? Oh, bother . . . My memory has shrunk in the washing. Well, we did give it a good rinsing, didn't we? Anyway, I gathered that somebody was collecting data for a book on Sebastian Knight. Funny, you don't seem to have—"

"Sebastian Knight?" said a sudden voice in the mist, "Who is speaking of Sebastian Knight?"

THE REAL LIFE OF
SEBASTIAN KNIGHT

THE stranger who uttered these words now approached—Oh, how I sometimes yearn for the easy swing of a well-oiled novel! How comfortable it would have been had the voice belonged to some cheery old don with long downy ear-lobes and that puckering about the eyes which stands for wisdom and humour . . . A handy character, a welcome passer-by who had also known my hero, but from a different angle. "And now," he would say, "I am going to tell you the real story of Sebastian Knight's college years." And then and there he would have launched on that story. But alas, nothing of the kind really happened. That Voice in the Mist rang out in the dimmest passage of my mind. It was but the echo of some possible truth, a timely reminder: don't be too certain of learning the past from the lips of the present. Beware of the most honest broker. Remember that what you are told is really threefold: shaped by the teller, reshaped by the listener, concealed from both by the dead man of the tale. Who is speaking of Sebastian Knight? repeats that voice in my conscience. Who indeed? His best friend and his half-brother. A gentle scholar, remote from life, and an embarrassed traveller visiting a distant land. And where is the third party? Rotting peacefully in the cemetery of St. Damier. Laughingly alive in five volumes. Peering unseen over my shoulder as I write this (although I dare say he mistrusted too strongly the commonplace of eternity to believe even now in his own ghost).

Anyway, here was I with the booty that friendship could yield. To this I added a few casual facts occurring in Sebastian's very short letters belonging to that period and the chance references to University life found scattered amongst his books. I then returned to London where I had neatly planned my next move.

At our last meeting Sebastian had happened to mention a kind of secretary whom he had employed from time to time between 1930 and 1934. Like many authors in the past, and as very few in the present (or perhaps we are simply unaware of those who fail to manage their affairs in a sound pushing manner), Sebastian was ridiculously helpless in business matters and once having found an adviser (who incidentally might be a shark or a blockhead—or both) he gave himself up to him entirely with the greatest relief. Had I perchance inquired whether he was perfectly certain that So-and-So now handling his affairs was not a meddlesome old rogue, he would have hurriedly changed the subject, so in dread was he that the discovery of another's mischief might force his own laziness into action. In a word he preferred the worst assistant to no assistant at all, and would convince himself and others that he was perfectly content with his choice. Having said all this I should like to stress the fact as definitely as possible that none of my words are—from a legal point of view— slanderous, and that the name I am about to mention has *not* appeared in this particular paragraph.

Now what I wanted from Mr. Goodman was not so much an account of Sebastian's last years—that I did not yet need —(for I intended to follow his life stage by stage without overtaking him), but merely to obtain a few suggestions as to what people I ought to see who might know something of Sebastian's post-Cambridge period.

So on March first, 1936, I called on Mr. Goodman at his office in Fleet Street. But before describing our interview I must be allowed a short digression.

Amongst Sebastian's letters I found as already mentioned some correspondence between him and his publisher dealing with a certain novel. It appears that in Sebastian's first book (1925), *The Prismatic Bezel*, one of the minor characters is an extremely comic and cruel skit upon a certain living author whom Sebastian found necessary to chastise. Naturally the publisher knew it immediately and this fact made him so uncomfortable that he advised Sebastian to modify the whole passage, a thing which Sebastian flatly refused to do, saying finally that he would get the book printed elsewhere,—and this he eventually did.

"You seem to wonder," he wrote in one letter, "what on earth could make me, a budding author (as you say—but that is a misapplied term, for your authentic budding author remains budding all his life; others, like me, spring into blossom in one bound), you seem to wonder, let me repeat (which does not mean I am apologising for that Proustian parenthesis), why the hell I should take a nice porcelain blue contemporary (X. does remind one, doesn't he, of those cheap china things which tempt one at fairs to an orgy of noisy destruction) and let him drop from the tower of my prose to the gutter below. You tell me he is widely esteemed; that his sales in Germany are almost as tremendous as his sales here; that an old story of his has just been selected for *Modern Masterpieces*; that together with Y. and Z. he is considered one of the leading writers of the 'post-war' generation; and that, last but not least, he is dangerous as a critic. You seem to hint that we should all keep the dark secret of his success, which is to travel second-class with a third-class ticket,—or if my simile is not sufficiently clear,—to pamper the taste of the worst category of the reading public—not those who revel in detective yarns, bless their pure souls—but those who buy the worst banalities because they have been shaken up in a modern way with a dash of Freud or 'stream of consciousness' or whatnot,—and incidentally do not and never will understand that the pretty cynics of to-day are Marie Corelli's nieces and old Mrs. Grundy's nephews. Why should we keep that shameful secret? What is this masonic bond of triteness—or indeed tritheism? Down with these shoddy gods! And then you go and tell me that my 'literary career' will be hopelessly handicapped from the start by my attacking an influential and esteemed writer. But even if there were such a thing as a 'literary career' and I were disqualified merely for riding my own horse, still I would refuse to change one single word in what I have written. For, believe me, no imminent punishment can be violent enough to make me abandon the pursuit of my pleasure, especially when this pleasure is the firm young bosom of truth. There are in fact not many things in life comparable to the delight of satire, and when I imagine the humbug's face as he reads (and read he shall) that particular passage and knows as well as we do that it is the truth, then delight reaches its sweetest climax. Let me add that if I have faithfully rendered not only X.'s inner world (which is no more than a tube-station during rush hours) but also his tricks of speech and demeanour, I emphatically deny that he or any other reader may discern the least trace of vulgarity in the passage which causes you such alarm. So do not let this haunt you any longer. Remember too that I take all responsibility, moral and commercial, in case you really 'get into trouble' with my innocent little volume."

My point in quoting this letter (apart from its own value as showing Sebastian in that bright boyish mood which later remained as a rainbow across the stormy gloom of his darkest tales) is to settle a rather delicate question. In a minute or two Mr. Goodman will appear in flesh and blood. The reader already knows how thoroughly I disapprove of that gentleman's book. However, at the time of our first (and last) interview I knew nothing about his work (insofar as a rapid compilation may be called work). I approached Mr. Goodman with an open mind; it is no longer open now, and naturally this is bound to influence my description. At the same time I do not very well see how I can discuss my visit to him without alluding even as discreetly as in the case of Sebastian's college-friend, to Mr. Goodman's manner if not appearance. Shall I be able to stop at that? Will not Mr. Goodman's face suddenly pop out to the owner's rightful annoyance when he reads these lines? I have studied Sebastian's letter and arrived at the conclusion that what Sebastian Knight might permit himself in respect to Mr. X. is denied me in regard to Mr. Goodman. The frankness of Sebastian's genius cannot be mine, and I should only succeed in being rude there where he might have been brilliant. So that I am treading on very thin ice and must try to step warily as I enter Mr. Goodman's study.

"Pray be seated," he said, courteously waving me into a leather armchair near his desk. He was remarkably well-dressed though decidedly with a city flavour. A black mask covered his face. "What can I do for you?" He went on looking at me through the eyeholes and still holding my card.

I suddenly realised that my name conveyed nothing to him. Sebastian had made his mother's name his own very completely.

"I am," I answered, "Sebastian Knight's half-brother." There was a short silence.

"Let me see," said Mr. Goodman, "am I to understand, that you are referring to the late Sebastian Knight, the well-known author?"

"Exactly," said I.

Mr. Goodman with finger and thumb stroked his face . . . I mean the face under his mask . . . stroked it down, down, reflectively.

"I beg your pardon," he said, "but are you quite sure that there is not some mistake?"

"None whatever," I replied, and in as few words as possible I explained my relationship to Sebastian.

"Oh, is that so?" said Mr. Goodman, growing more and more pensive. "Really, really, it never entered my head. I was certainly quite aware that Knight was born and brought up in Russia. But I somehow missed the point about his name. Yes, now I see . . . Yes, it ought to be a Russian one . . . His mother . . ."

Mr. Goodman drummed the blotting-pad for a minute with his fine white fingers and then faintly sighed.

"Well, what's done is done," he remarked. "Too late now to add a . . . I mean," he hurriedly continued, "that I'm sorry not to have gone into the matter before. So you are his half-brother? Well, I am delighted to meet you."

"First of all," I said, "I should like to settle the business-question. Mr. Knight's papers, at least those that refer to his literary occupations, are not in very great order and I don't quite know exactly how things stand. I haven't yet seen his publishers, but I gather that at least one of them—the firm that brought out *The Funny Mountain*—no longer exists. Before going further into the matter I thought I'd better have a talk with you."

"Quite so," said Mr. Goodman. "As a matter of fact you may not be cognizant of my having interest in two Knight books, *The Funny Mountain* and *Lost Property*. Under the circumstances the best thing would be for me to give you some details which I can send you by letter to-morrow morning as well as a copy of my contract with Mr. Knight. Or should I call him Mr. . . ." and smiling under his mask Mr. Goodman tried to pronounce our simple Russian name.

"Then there is another matter," I continued. "I have decided to write a book on his life and work, and I sorely need certain information. Could you perhaps . . ."

It seemed to me that Mr. Goodman stiffened. Then he coughed once or twice and even went as far as to select a black-currant lozenge from a small box on his distinguished-looking desk.

"My dear Sir," he said, suddenly veering together with his seat and whirling his eyeglass on his ribbon. "Let us be perfectly outspoken. I have certainly known poor Knight better than anyone else, but . . . look here, have you started writing that book?"

"No," I said.

"Then don't. You must excuse my being so very blunt. An old habit,—a bad habit, perhaps. You don't mind, do you? Well, what I mean is . . . how should I put it? . . . You see,

Sebastian Knight was not what you might call a great writer
... Oh, yes, I know,—a fine artist and all that,—but with no
appeal to the general public. I don't wish to say that a book
could not be written about him. It could. But then it ought
to be written from a special point of view which would make
the subject fascinating. Otherwise it is bound to fall flat,
because, you see, I really don't think that Sebastian Knight's
fame is strong enough to sustain anything like the work you
are contemplating."

I was so taken aback by this outburst that I kept silent.
And Mr. Goodman went on:

"I trust my bluntness does not offend you. Your half-
brother and I were such good pals that you quite understand
how I feel about it. Better not, my dear sir, better not. Leave
it to some professional fellow, to one who knows the book-
market—and he will tell you that anybody trying to complete
an exhaustive study of Knight's life and work, as you put it,
would be wasting his and the reader's time. Why, even So-
and-So's book about the late . . . [a famous name was men-
tioned] with all those photographs and facsimiles did not
sell."

I thanked Mr. Goodman for his advice and reached for my
hat. I felt he had proved a failure and that I had followed a
false scent. Somehow or other I did not care to ask him to
enlarge upon those days when he and Sebastian had been
"such pals." I wonder now what his answer would have been
had I begged him to tell me the story of his secretaryship.
After shaking hands with me most cordially, he returned the
black mask which I pocketed, as I supposed it might come in
usefully on some other occasion. He saw me to the nearest
glass door and there we parted. As I was about to go down

the stairs, a vigourous-looking girl whom I had noticed steadily typing in one of the rooms ran after me and stopped me (queer,—that Sebastian's Cambridge friend had also called me back).

"My name," she said, "is Helen Pratt. I have overheard as much of your conversation as I could stand and there is a little thing I want to ask you. Clare Bishop is a great friend of mine. There's something she wants to find out. Could I talk to you one of these days?"

I said yes, most certainly, and we fixed the time.

"I knew Mr. Knight quite well," she added, looking at me with bright round eyes.

"Oh, really," said I, not quite knowing what else to say.

"Yes," she went on, "he was an amazing personality, and I don't mind telling you that I loathed Goodman's book about him."

"What do you mean?" I asked. "What book?"

"Oh, the one he has just written. I was going over the proofs with him this last week. Well, I must be running. Thank you so much."

She darted away and very slowly I descended the steps. Mr. Goodman's large soft pinkish face was, and is, remarkably like a cow's udder.

THE REAL LIFE OF SEBASTIAN KNIGHT

MR. GOODMAN'S book *The Trag-edy of Sebastian Knight* has enjoyed a very good press. It has been lengthily reviewed in the leading dailies and week-lies. It has been called "impressive and convincing." The au-thor has been credited with "deep insight" into an "essen-tially modern" character. Passages have been quoted to demonstrate his efficient handling of nutshells. One critic even went as far as to take his hat off to Mr. Goodman—who, let it be added, had used his own merely to talk through it. In a word, Mr. Goodman has been patted on the back when he ought to have been rapped on the knuckles.

I, for one, would have ignored that book altogether had it been just another bad book, doomed with the rest of its kind to oblivion by next spring. The Lethean Library, for all its incalculable volumes, is, I know, sadly incomplete without Mr. Goodman's effort. But bad as the book may be, it is something else besides. Owing to the quality of its subject, it is bound to become quite mechanically the satellite of an-other man's enduring fame. As long as Sebastian Knight's name is remembered, there always will be some learned in-quirer conscientiously climbing up a ladder to where *The Tragedy of Sebastian Knight* keeps half awake between God-frey Goodman's *Fall of Man* and Samuel Goodrich's *Recol-lections of a Lifetime*. Thus, if I continue to harp on the sub-ject, I do so for Sebastian Knight's sake.

Mr. Goodman's method is as simple as his philosophy. His sole object is to show "poor Knight" as a product and victim of what he calls "our time"—though why some people are so keen to make others share in their chronometric concepts, has always been a mystery to me. "Postwar Unrest," "Postwar Generation" are to Mr. Goodman magic words opening every door. There is, however, a certain kind of "open sesame" which seems less a charm than a skeleton-key, and this, I am afraid, is Mr. Goodman's kind. But he is quite wrong in thinking that he found something once the lock had been forced. Not that I wish to suggest that Mr. Goodman *thinks*. He could not if he tried. His book concerns itself only with such ideas as have been shown (commercially) to attract mediocre minds.

For Mr. Goodman, young Sebastian Knight "freshly emerged from the carved chrysalid of Cambridge" is a youth of acute sensibility in a cruel cold world. In this world, "outside realities intrude so roughly upon one's most intimate dreams" that a young man's soul is forced into a state of siege before it is finally shattered. "The War," says Mr. Goodman without so much as a blush, "had changed the face of the universe." And with much gusto he goes on to describe those special aspects of postwar life which met a young man at "the troubled dawn of his career": a feeling of some great deception; weariness of the soul and feverish physical excitement (such as the "vapid lewdness of the fox-trot"); a sense of futility—and its result: gross liberty. Cruelty, too; the reek of blood still in the air; glaring picture-palaces; dim couples in dark Hyde Park; the glories of standardisation; the cult of machinery; the degradation of Beauty, Love, Honour, Art . . . and so on. It is really a wonder that Mr. Goodman himself who, as far as I know, was Sebastian's coeval, managed to live through those terrific years.

But what Mr. Goodman could stand, his Sebastian Knight apparently could not. We are given a picture of Sebastian restlessly pacing the rooms of his London flat in 1923, after a short trip to the Continent, which Continent "shocked him indescribably by the vulgar glamour of its gambling-hells." Yes, "pacing up and down . . . clutching at his temples . . . in a passion of discontent . . . angry with the world . . . alone . . . eager to do something, but weak, weak . . ." The dots are not Mr. Goodman's tremolos, but denote sentences I have kindly left out. "No," Mr. Goodman goes on, "this was not the world for an artist to live in. It was all very well to flaunt a brave countenance, to make a great display of that cynicism which so irritates one in Knight's earlier work and so pains one in his last two volumes . . . it was all very well to appear contemptuous and ultrasophisticated, but the thorn was there, the sharp, poisonous thorn." I don't know why, but the presence of this (perfectly mythical) thorn seems to give Mr. Goodman a grim satisfaction.

It would be unfair of me if I let it seem that this first chapter of *The Tragedy of Sebastian Knight* consists exclusively of a thick flow of philosophical treacle. Word-pictures and anecdotes which form the body of the book (that is, when Mr. Goodman arrives at the stage of Sebastian's life when he met him personally) appear here too, as rockcakes dotting the syrup. Mr. Goodman was no Boswell; still, no doubt, he kept a note-book where he jotted down certain remarks of his employer—and apparently some of these related to his employer's past. In other words, we must imagine that Sebastian in between work would say: Do you know, my dear Goodman, this reminds me of a day in my life, some years ago, when ... Here would come the story. Half a dozen of these seem to Mr. Goodman sufficient to fill out what is to him a blank—Sebastian's youth in England.

The first of these stories (which Mr. Goodman considers to be extremely typical of "postwar undergraduate life") depicts Sebastian showing a girl-friend from London the sights of Cambridge. "And this is the Dean's window," he said; then smashing the pane with a stone, he added: "And this is the Dean." Needless to say that Sebastian has been pulling Mr. Goodman's leg: the story is as old as the University itself.

Let us look at the second one. During a short vacation trip to Germany (1921? 1922?) Sebastian, one night, being annoyed by the caterwauls in the street, started to pelt the offenders with miscellaneous objects including an egg. Presently, a policeman knocked at his door, bringing back all these objects minus the egg.

This is from an old (or, as Mr. Goodman would say, "prewar") Jerome K. Jerome book. Leg-pulling again.

Third story: Sebastian speaking of his very first novel (unpublished and destroyed) explained that it was about a fat young student who travels home to find his mother married to his uncle; this uncle, an ear-specialist, had murdered the student's father.

Mr. Goodman misses the joke.

Fourth: Sebastian in the summer of 1922 had overworked himself and, suffering from hallucinations, used to see a kind of optical ghost,—a black-robed monk moving swiftly towards him from the sky.

This is a little harder: a short story by Chekhov.
Fifth:
But I think we had better stop, or else Mr. Goodman might be in danger of becoming a centipede. Let us have him remain quadrupedal. I am sorry for him, but it cannot be helped. And if only he had not padded and commented these "curious incidents and fancies" so ponderously, with such a rich crop of deductions! Churlish, capricious, mad Sebastian, struggling in a naughty world of Juggernauts, and aeronauts, and naughts, and what-nots . . . Well, well, there may be something in all that.

I want to be scientifically precise. I should hate being balked of the tiniest particle of truth only because at a certain point of my search I was blindly enraged by a trashy concoction . . . Who is speaking of Sebastian Knight? His former secretary. Were they ever friends? No,—as we shall see later. Is there anything real or possible in the contrast between a frail eager Sebastian and a wicked tired world? Not a thing. Was there perhaps some other kind of chasm, breach, fissure? There was.

It is enough to turn to the first thirty pages or so of *Lost Property* to see how blandly Mr. Goodman (who incidentally never quotes anything that may clash with the main idea of his fallacious work) misunderstands Sebastian's inner attitude in regard to the outer world. Time for Sebastian was never 1914 or 1920 or 1936—it was always year 1. Newspaper headlines, political theories, fashionable ideas meant to him no more than the loquacious printed notice (in three languages, with mistakes in at least two) on the wrapper of some soap or toothpaste. The lather might be thick and the notice convincing—but that was an end of it. He could perfectly well understand sensitive and intelligent thinkers not being able to sleep because of an earthquake in China; but, being what he was, he could not understand why these same people did not feel exactly the same spasm of rebellious grief when thinking of some similar calamity that had happened as many years ago as there were miles to China. Time and space were to him measures of the same eternity, so that the very idea of his reacting in any special "modern" way to what Mr. Goodman calls "the atmosphere of postwar Europe" is utterly preposterous. He was intermittently happy and uncomfortable in the world into which he came, just as a traveller may be exhilarated by visions of his voyage and be almost simultaneously sea-sick. Whatever age Sebastian might have been born in, he would have been equally amused and unhappy, joyful and apprehensive, as a child at a pantomime now and then thinking of to-morrow's dentist. And the reason of his discomfort was not that he was moral in an immoral age, or immoral in a moral one, neither was it the cramped feeling of his youth not blowing naturally enough in a world which was too rapid a succession of funerals and fireworks; it was simply his becoming aware that the rhythm of his inner being was so much richer than that of other souls. Even then, just at the close of his Cambridge period, and perhaps earlier too, he knew that his slightest thought or sensation had always at least one more dimension than those of his neighbours. He might have boasted of this had there been anything lurid in his nature. As there was not, it only remained for him to feel the awkwardness of being a crystal among glass, a sphere among circles (but all this was nothing when compared to what he experienced as he finally settled down to his literary task).

"I was," writes Sebastian in *Lost Property*, "so shy that I always managed somehow to commit the fault I was most anxious to avoid. In my disastrous attempt to match the colour of my surroundings I could only be compared to a colour-blind chameleon. My shyness would have been easier to bear—for me and for others—had it been of the normal clammy-and-pimply kind: many a young fellow passes through this stage and nobody really minds. But with me it assumed a morbid secret form which had nothing to do with the throes of puberty. Among the most hackneyed inventions of the torture house there is one consisting of denying the prisoner sleep. Most people live through the day with this or that part of their mind in a happy state of somnolence: a hungry man eating a steak is interested in his food and not, say, in the memory of a dream about angels wearing top-hats which he happened to see seven years ago; but in my case all the shutters and lids and doors of the mind would be open at once at all times of the day. Most brains have their Sundays, mine was even refused a half-holiday. This state of constant wakefulness was extremely painful not only in itself, but in its direct results. Every ordinary act which, as a matter of course, I had to perform, took on such a complicated appearance, provoked such a multitude of associative ideas in my mind, and these associations were so tricky and obscure, so utterly useless for practical application, that I would either shirk the business at hand or else make a mess of it out of sheer nervousness. When one morning I went to see the editor of a review who, I thought, might print some of my Cambridge poems, a particular stammer he had, blending with a certain combination of angles in the pattern of roofs and chimneys, all slightly distorted owing to a flaw in the glass of the window-pane,—this and a queer musty smell in the room (of roses rotting in the waste-paper basket?) sent my thoughts on such long and intricate errands that, instead of saying what I had meant to say, I suddenly started telling this man whom I was seeing for the first time, about the literary plans of a mutual friend, who, I remembered too late, had asked me to keep them secret . . .

". . . Knowing, as I did, the dangerous vagrancies of my consciousness I was afraid of meeting people, of hurting their feelings or making myself ridiculous in their eyes. But this same quality or defect which tormented me so, when confronted with what is called the practical side of life (though, between you and me, bookkeeping or bookselling looks singularly unreal in the starlight), became an instrument of exquisite pleasure whenever I yielded to my loneliness. I was deeply in love with the country which was my home (as far as my nature could afford the notion of home); I had my Kipling moods and my Rupert Brooke moods, and my Housman moods. The blind man's dog near Harrods or a pavement-artist's coloured chalks; brown leaves in a New Forest ride or a tin bath hanging outside on the black brick wall of a slum; a picture in Punch or a purple passage in Hamlet, all went to form a definite harmony, where I, too, had the shadow of a place. My memory of the London of my youth is the memory of endless vague wanderings, of a sun-dazzled window suddenly piercing the blue morning mist or of beautiful black wires with suspended raindrops running along them. I seem to pass with intangible steps across ghostly lawns and through dancing-halls full of the whine of Hawaiian music and down dear drab little streets with pretty names, until I come to a certain warm hollow where something very like the selfest of my own self sits huddled up in the darkness."

It is a pity Mr. Goodman had not the leisure to peruse this passage, though it is doubtful whether he would have grasped its inner meaning.

He was kind enough to send me a copy of his work. In the letter accompanying it he explained in heavily bantering tones, with what was epistolarily meant to be a good-natured wink, that if he had not mentioned the book in the course of our interview, it was because he wanted it to be a splendid surprise. His tone, his guffaws, his pompous wit—all this suggested an old gruff friend of the family turning up with a precious gift for the youngest. But Mr. Goodman is not a very good actor. Not for a moment did he really think that I would be delighted either with the book he wrote or with the mere fact that he had gone out of his way to advertise the name of a member of my family. He knew all along that his book was rubbish, and he knew that neither its binding, nor its jacket, nor the blurb on the jacket, nor indeed any of the reviews and notices in the press would deceive me. Why he had considered it wiser to keep me in the dark is not quite evident. Perhaps he thought I might wickedly sit down and dash off my own volume, just in time to have it collide with his.

But he not only sent me his book. He also produced the account he had promised me. This is not the place to discuss these matters. I have handed them over to my solicitor who has already acquainted me with his conclusions. Here I may only say that Sebastian's candour in practical affairs was taken advantage of in the coarsest fashion. Mr. Goodman has never been a regular literary agent. He has only bet on books. He does not rightfully belong to that intelligent, honest and hardworking profession. We will leave it at that; but I have not yet done with *The Tragedy of Sebastian Knight* or rather—*The Farce of Mr. Goodman.*

THE REAL LIFE OF
SEBASTIAN KNIGHT

TWO years had elapsed after my mother's death before I saw Sebastian again. One picture postcard was all I had had from him during that time, except the cheques he insisted on sending me. On a dull gray afternoon in November or December, 1924, as I was walking up the Champs Elysées towards the Etoile I suddenly caught sight of Sebastian through the glass front of a popular café. I remember my first impulse was to continue on my way, so pained was I by the sudden revelation that having arrived in Paris he had not communicated with me. Then on second thought I entered. I saw the back of Sebastian's glossy dark head and the downcast bespectacled face of the girl sitting opposite him. She was reading a letter which, as I approached, she handed back to him with a faint smile and took off her horn-rimmed glasses.

"Isn't it rich?" asked Sebastian, and at the same moment I laid my hand on his thin shoulder.

"Oh, hullo, V.," he said looking up. "This is my brother, Miss Bishop. Sit down and make yourself comfortable." She was pretty in a quiet sort of way with a pale faintly freckled complexion, slightly hollowed cheeks, blue-gray near-sighted eyes, a thin mouth. She wore a gray tailor-made with a blue scarf and a small three-cornered hat. I believe her hair was bobbed.

"I was just going to ring you up," said Sebastian, not very

truthfully I am afraid. "You see I am only here for the day and going back to London to-morrow. What will you have?"

They were drinking coffee. Clare Bishop, her lashes beating, rummaged in her bag, found her handkerchief, and dabbed first one pink nostril and then the other. "Cold getting worse," she said and clicked her bag.

"Oh, splendidly," said Sebastian, in reply to an obvious question. "As a matter of fact I have just finished writing a novel, and the publisher I've chosen seems to like it judging by his encouraging letter. He even seems to approve of the title *Cock Robin Hits Back* though Clare doesn't."

"I think it sounds silly," said Clare, "and besides a bird can't hit."

"It alludes to a well-known nursery-rhyme," said Sebastian, for my benefit.

"A silly allusion," said Clare; "your first title was much better."

"I don't know . . . The prism . . . The prismatic edge . . ." murmured Sebastian, "that's not quite what I want . . . Pity Cock Robin is so unpopular. . . ."

"A title," said Clare, "must convey the colour of the book, —not its subject."

It was the first time and also the last that I ever heard Sebastian discuss literary matters in my presence. Rarely, too, had I seen him in such a lighthearted mood. He appeared well-groomed and fit. His finely-shaped white face with that slight shading on the cheeks—he was one of those unfortunate men who have to shave twice a day when dining out —did not show a trace of that dull unhealthy tinge it so often had. His rather large slightly pointed ears were aflame as they were when he was pleasurably excited. I, for my part,

72

was tongue-tied and stiff. Somehow, I felt that I had barged in.

"Shall we go to a cinema or something," asked Sebastian diving into his waistcoat pocket, with two fingers.

"Just as you like," said Clare.

"Gah-song," said Sebastian. I had noticed before that he tried to pronounce French as a real healthy Britisher would.

For some time we searched under the table and under the plush seats for one of Clare's gloves. She used a nice cool perfume. At last I retrieved it, a gray suede glove with a white lining and a fringed gauntlet. She put them on leisurely as we pushed through the revolving door. Rather tall, very straight-backed, good ankles, flat-heeled shoes.

"Look here," I said, "I don't think I can go with you to the pictures. I'm dreadfully sorry, but I have got some things to attend to. Perhaps . . . But when exactly are you leaving?"

"Oh, to-night," replied Sebastian, "but I'll soon be over again . . . Stupid of me not to have let you know earlier. At any rate we can walk with you a little way . . ."

"Do you know Paris well?" I asked of Clare. . . .

"My parcel," she said stopping short.

"Oh, all right, I'll fetch it," said Sebastian and went back to the café.

We two proceeded very slowly up the wide sidewalk. I lamely repeated my question.

"Yes, fairly," she said. "I've got friends here—I'm staying with them until Christmas."

"Sebastian looks remarkably well," I said.

"Yes, I suppose he does," said Clare looking over her shoulder and then blinking at me. "When I first met him he looked a doomed man."

"When was that," I probably asked, for now I remember her answer: "This spring in London at a dreadful party, but then he always looks doomed at parties."

"Here are your bongs-bongs," said Sebastian's voice behind us. I told them I was going to the Etoile underground station and we skirted the place from the left. As we were about to cross the Avenue Kleber, Clare nearly got knocked down by a bicycle.

"You little fool," said Sebastian, gripping her by the elbow.

"Far too many pigeons," she said, as we reached the curb.

"Yes, and they smell," added Sebastian.

"What kind of smell? My nose is stuffed up," she asked sniffing and peering at the dense crowd of fat birds strutting about our feet.

"Iris and rubber," said Sebastian.

The groan of a motor-lorry in the act of avoiding a furniture-van sent the birds wheeling across the sky. They settled among the pearl-gray and black frieze of the Arc de Triomphe and when some of them fluttered off again it seemed as if bits of the carved entablature were turned into flaky life. A few years later I found that picture, "that stone melting into wing," in Sebastian's third book.

We crossed more avenues and then came to the white banisters of the underground station. Here we parted, quite cheerfully . . . I remember Sebastian's receding raincoat and Clare's blue-gray figure. She took his arm and altered her step to fall in with his swinging stride.

Now, I learnt from Miss Pratt a number of things which made me wish to learn a good deal more. Her object in applying to me was to find out whether any of Clare Bishop's letters to Sebastian had remained among his things. She stressed the point that it was not Clare Bishop's commission; that in fact Clare Bishop knew nothing of our interview. She had been married now for three or four years and was much too proud to speak of the past. Miss Pratt had seen her a week or so after Sebastian's death had got into the papers, but although the two women were very old friends (that is, knew more about each other than each of them thought the other knew) Clare did not dwell upon the event.

"I hope he was not too unhappy," she said quietly and then added, "I wonder if he kept my letters?"

The way she said this, the narrowing of her eyes, the quick sigh she gave before changing the subject, convinced her friend that it would be a great relief for her to know the letters had been destroyed. I asked Miss Pratt whether I could get in touch with Clare; whether Clare might be coaxed into talking to me about Sebastian. Miss Pratt answered that knowing Clare she would not even dare to transmit my request. "Hopeless," was what she said. For a moment I was basely tempted to hint that I had the letters in my keeping and would hand them over to Clare provided she granted me a personal interview, so passionate was my longing to meet her, just to see and to watch the shadow of the name I would mention flit across her face. But no,—I could not blackmail Sebastian's past. That was out of the question.

"The letters are burnt," I said. I then continued to plead, repeating again and again that surely there could be no harm in trying; could she not convince Clare, when telling her of our talk, that my visit would be very short, very innocent?

"What is it exactly you want to know?" asked Miss Pratt, "because, you see, I can tell you lots myself."

She spoke for a long time about Clare and Sebastian. She

did it very well, although, like most women, she was inclined to be somewhat didactic in retrospection.

"Do you mean to say," I interrupted her at a certain point of her story, "that nobody ever found out what that other woman's name was?"

"No," said Miss Pratt.

"But how shall I find her," I cried.

"You never will."

"When do you say it began?" I interrupted again, as she referred to his illness.

"Well," she said, "I'm not quite sure. What I witnessed wasn't his first attack. We were coming out of some restaurant. It was very cold and he could not find a taxi. He got nervous and angry. He started to run towards one that had drawn up a little way off. Then he stopped and said he was not feeling well. I remember he took a pill or something out of a little box and crushed it in his white silk scarf, sort of pressing it to his face as he did so. That must have been in twenty-seven or twenty-eight."

I asked several more questions. She answered them all in the same conscientious fashion and went on with her dismal tale.

When she had gone, I wrote it all down—but it was dead, dead. I simply had to see Clare! One glance, one word, the mere sound of her voice would be sufficient (and necessary, absolutely necessary) to animate the past. Why it was thus I did not understand, just as I have never understood why on a certain unforgettable day some weeks earlier I had been so sure that if I could find a dying man alive and conscious I would learn something which no human being had yet learnt.

Then one Monday morning I made a call.

The maid showed me into a small sitting-room. Clare was at home, this at least I learnt from that ruddy and rather raw young female. (Sebastian mentions somewhere that English novelists never depart from a certain fixed tone when describing housemaids.) On the other hand I knew from Miss Pratt that Mr. Bishop was busy in the City on weekdays; queer—her having married a man with the same name, no relation either, just pure coincidence. Would she not see me? Fairly well off, I should say, but not very . . . Probably an L-shaped drawing room on the first floor and over that a couple of bedrooms. The whole street consisted of just such close-pressed narrow houses. She was long in making up her mind . . . Should I have risked telephoning first? Had Miss Pratt already told her about the letters? Suddenly I heard soft footfalls coming down the stairs and a huge man in a black dressing-gown with purple facings came bouncing into the room.

"I apologise for my attire," he said, "but I am suffering from a severe cold. My name is Bishop and I gather you want to see my wife."

Had he caught that cold, I thought in a curious flash of fancy, from the pink nosed husky voiced Clare I had seen twelve years ago?

"Why, yes," I said, "if she hasn't forgotten me. We met once in Paris."

"Oh, she remembered your name all right," said Mr. Bishop, looking at me squarely, "but I am sorry to say she can't see you."

"May I call later?" I asked.

There was a slight silence, and then Mr. Bishop asked.

"Am I right in presuming that your visit is connected in

some way with your brother's death?" There he stood before me, hands thrust into his dressing-gown pockets, looking at me, his fair hair brushed back with an angry brush—a good fellow, a decent fellow, and I hope he will not mind my saying so here. Quite recently, I may add, in very sad circumstances, letters have been exchanged between us, which have quite done away with any ill-feeling that might have crept into our first conversation.

"Would that prevent her seeing me?" I asked in my turn. It was a foolish phrase, I admit.

"You are not going to see her in any case," said Mr. Bishop. "Sorry," he added, relenting a little, as he felt I was safely drifting out. "I am sure that in other circumstances . . . but you see my wife is not overkeen to recall past friendships, and you will forgive me if I say quite frankly I do not think you should have come."

I walked back feeling I had bungled it badly. I pictured to myself what I would have said to Clare had I found her alone. Somehow I managed to convince myself now that had she been alone, she would have seen me: so an unforeseen obstacle belittles those one had imagined. I would have said: "Let us not talk of Sebastian. Let us talk of Paris. Do you know it well? Do you remember those pigeons? Tell me what have you been reading lately . . . And what about films? Do you still lose your gloves, parcels?" Or else I might have resorted to a bolder method, a direct attack. "Yes, I know how you must feel about it, but please, please, talk to me about him. For the sake of his portrait. For the sake of little things which will wander away and perish if you refuse to let me have them for my book about him." Oh, I was sure she would never have refused.

And two days later with this last intention firm in my mind, I made still another attempt. This time I was resolved to be much more circumspect. It was a fine morning, quite early yet, and I was sure she would not stay indoors. I would unobtrusively take up my position at the corner of her street, wait for her husband's departure to the City, wait for her to come out and then accost her. But things did not work out quite as I had expected.

I had still some little way to go when suddenly Clare Bishop appeared. She had just crossed from my side of the street to the opposite pavement. I knew her at once although I had seen her only for a short half-hour years before. I knew her although her face was now pinched and her body strangely full. She walked slowly and heavily, and as I crossed towards her I realised that she was in an advanced stage of pregnancy. Owing to the impetuous strain in my nature, which has often led me astray, I found myself walking towards her with a smile of welcome, but in those few instants I was already overwhelmed by the perfectly clear consciousness that I might neither talk to her nor greet her in any manner. It had nothing to do with Sebastian or my book, or my words with Mr. Bishop, it was solely on account of her stately concentration. I knew I was forbidden even to make myself known to her, but as I say my impetus had carried me across the street and in such a way that I nearly bumped into her upon reaching the pavement. She sidestepped heavily and lifted her near-sighted eyes. No, thank God, she did not recognise me. There was something heartrending in the solemn expression of her pale sawdusty face. We had both stopped short. With ridiculous presence of mind I brought out of my pocket the first thing my hand met with, and I said: "I beg your pardon, but have you dropped this?"

"No," she said, with an impersonal smile. She held it for a moment close to her eyes, "no," she repeated, and giving it back to me went on her way. I stood with a key in my hand, as if I had just picked it up off the pavement. It was the latch-key of Sebastian's flat, and with a queer pang I now realised that she had touched it with her innocent blind fingers. . . .

THE REAL LIFE OF
SEBASTIAN KNIGHT

THEIR relationship lasted six years.
During that period Sebastian produced his two first novels:
The Prismatic Bezel and *Success*. It took him some seven
months to compose the first (April-October, 1924) and
twenty-two months to compose the second (July, 1925-
April, 1927). Between autumn, 1927, and summer, 1929, he
wrote the three stories which later (1932) were re-published
together under the title *The Funny Mountain*. In other words,
Clare intimately witnessed the first three fifths of his entire
production (I skip the juvenilia—the Cambridge poems for
instance—which he himself destroyed); and as in the intervals between the above-mentioned books Sebastian kept
twisting and laying aside and re-twisting this or that imaginative scheme it may be safely assumed that during those six
years he was continuously occupied. And Clare loved his
occupation.

She entered his life without knocking, as one might step
into the wrong room because of its vague resemblance to
one's own. She stayed there forgetting the way out and
quietly getting used to the strange creatures she found there
and petted despite their amazing shapes. She had no special
intention of being happy or of making Sebastian happy, nor
had she the slightest misgivings as to what might come next;
it was merely a matter of naturally accepting life with Sebastian because life without him was less imaginable than a tel-

lurian's camping-tent on a mountain in the moon. Most probably, if she had borne him a child they would have slipped into marriage since that would have been the simplest way for all three; but that not being the case it did not enter their heads to submit to those white and wholesome formalities which very possibly both would have enjoyed had they given them necessary thought. There was nothing of your advanced prejudice-be-damned stuff about Sebastian. Well did he know that to flaunt one's contempt for a moral code was but smuggled smugness and prejudice turned inside out. He usually chose the easiest ethical path (just as he chose the thorniest aesthetic one) merely because it happened to be the shortest cut to his chosen object; he was far too lazy in everyday life (just as he was far too hardworking in his artistic life) to be bothered by problems set and solved by others.

Clare was twenty-two when she met Sebastian. She did not remember her father; her mother was dead too, and her stepfather had married again, so that the faint notion of home which that couple presented to her might be compared to the old sophism of changed handle and changed blade, though of course she could hardly expect to find and join the original parts—this side of Eternity at least. She lived alone in London, rather vaguely attending an art school and taking a course in Eastern languages, of all things. People liked her because she was quietly attractive with her charming dim face and soft husky voice, somehow remaining in one's memory as if she were subtly endowed with the gift of being remembered: she came out well in one's mind, she was mnemogenic. Even her rather large and knuckly hands had a singular charm, and she was a good light silent dancer. But best of all she was one of those rare, very rare women who do not take the world for granted and who see everyday things not merely as familiar mirrors of their own feminity. She had imagination—the muscle of the soul—and her imagination was of a particularly strong, almost masculine quality. She possessed, too, that real sense of beauty which has far less to do with art than with the constant readiness to discern the halo round a frying-pan or the likeness between a weeping-willow and a Skye terrier. And finally she was blest with a keen sense of humour. No wonder she fitted into his life so well.

Already during the first season of their acquaintance they saw a great deal of each other; in the autumn she went to Paris and he visited her there more than once, I suspect. By then his first book was ready. She had learnt to type and the summer evenings of 1924 had been to her as many pages slipped into the slit and rolled out again alive with black and violet words. I should like to imagine her tapping the glistening keys to the sound of a warm shower rustling in the dark elms beyond the open window, with Sebastian's slow and serious voice (he did not merely dictate, said Miss Pratt,—he officiated) coming and going across the room. He used to spend most of the day writing, but so labourious was his progress that there would hardly be more than a couple of fresh pages for her to type in the evening and even these had to be done over again, for Sebastian used to indulge in an orgy of corrections; and sometimes he would do what I daresay no author ever did—recopy the typed sheet in his own slanting un-English hand and then dictate it anew. His struggle with words was unusually painful and this for two reasons. One was the common one with writers of his type: the bridging of the abyss lying between expression and thought; the maddening feeling that the right words, the only words are awaiting you on the opposite bank in the misty distance, and the shudderings of the still unclothed thought clamouring for them on this side of the abyss. He had no use for ready-made phrases because the things he wanted to say were of an exceptional build and he knew moreover that no real idea can be said to exist without the words made to measure. So that (to use a closer simile) the thought which only seemed naked was but pleading for the clothes it wore to become visible, while the words lurking afar were not empty shells as they seemed, but were only waiting for the thought they already concealed to set them aflame and in motion. At times he felt like a child given a farrago of wires and ordered to produce the wonder of light. And he did produce it; and sometimes he would not be conscious at all of the way he succeeded in doing so, and at other times he would be worrying the wires for hours in what seemed the most rational way—and achieve nothing. And Clare, who had not composed a single line of imaginative prose or poetry in her life, understood so well (and that was her private miracle) every detail of Sebastian's struggle, that the words she typed were to her not so much the conveyors of their natural sense, but the curves and gaps and zigzags showing Sebastian's groping along a certain ideal line of expression.

This, however, was not all. I know, I know as definitely as I know we had the same father, I know Sebastian's Russian was better and more natural to him than his English. I quite believe that by not speaking Russian for five years he may have forced himself into thinking he had forgotten it. But a language is a live physical thing which cannot be so easily dismissed. It should moreover be remembered that five years before his first book—that is, at the time he left Russia,—his English was as thin as mine. I have improved mine artificially years later (by dint of hard study abroad); he tried to let his thrive naturally in its own surroundings. It did thrive wonderfully but still I maintain that had he started to write in Russian, those particular linguistic throes would have been spared him. Let me add that I have in my possession a letter written by him not long before his death. And that short letter is couched in a Russian purer and richer than his English ever was, no matter what beauty of expression he attained in his books.

I know too that as Clare took down the words he disentangled from his manuscript she sometimes would stop tapping and say with a little frown, slightly lifting the outer edge of the imprisoned sheet and re-reading the line: "No, my dear. You can't say it so in English." He would stare at her for an instant or two and then resume his prowl, reluctantly pondering on her observation, while she sat with her hands softly folded in her lap quietly waiting. "There is no other way of expressing it," he would mutter at last. "And if for instance," she would say—and then an exact suggestion would follow.

"Oh, well, if you like," he would reply.

"I'm not insisting, my dear, just as you wish, if you think bad grammar won't hurt . . ."

"Oh, go on," he would cry, "you are perfectly right, go on . . ."

By November, 1924, *The Prismatic Bezel* was completed. It was published in the following March and fell completely flat. As far as I can find out by looking up newspapers of that period, it was alluded to only once. Five lines and a half in a Sunday paper, between other lines referring to other books. *"The Prismatic Bezel* is apparently a first novel and as such ought not to be judged as severely as (So-and-So's book mentioned previously). Its fun seemed to me obscure and its obscurities funny, but possibly there exists a kind of fiction the niceties of which will always elude me. However, for the benefit of readers who like that sort of stuff I may add that Mr. Knight is as good at splitting hairs as he is at splitting infinitives."

That spring was probably the happiest period of Sebastian's existence. He had been delivered of one book and was already feeling the throbs of the next one. He was in excellent health. He had a delightful companion. He suffered from none of those petty worries which formerly used to assail him at times with the perseverance of a swarm of ants spreading over a hacienda. Clare posted letters for him, and checked laundry returns, and saw that he was well supplied with shaving blades, tobacco and salted almonds for which he had a special weakness. He enjoyed dining out with her and then going to a play. The play almost invariably made him writhe and groan afterwards, but he derived a morbid pleasure from dissecting platitudes. An expression of greed, of wicked eagerness, would make his nostrils expand while his back teeth ground in a paroxysm of disgust, as he pounced upon some poor triviality. Miss Pratt remembered one particular occasion when her father, who had at one time had some financial interest in the cinema industry, invited Sebastian and Clare to the private view of a very gorgeous and expensive film. The leading actor was a remarkably handsome young man wearing a luxurious turban and the plot was powerfully dramatic. At the highest point of tension, Sebastian, to Mr. Pratt's extreme surprise and annoyance, began to shake with laughter, with Clare bubbling too but plucking at his sleeve in a helpless effort to make him stop. They must have had a glorious time together, those two. And it is hard to believe that the warmth, the tenderness, the beauty of it has not been gathered, and is not treasured somewhere, somehow, by some immortal witness of mortal life. They must have been seen wandering in Kew Gardens, or Richmond Park (personally I have never been there but the names attract me), or eating ham and eggs at some pretty inn in their summer rambles in the country, or reading on the vast divan in Sebastian's study with the fire cheerfully burning and an English Christmas already filling the air with faintly spicy smells on a background of lavender and leather. And Sebastian must have been overheard telling her of the extraordinary things he would try to express in his next book *Success.*

One day in the summer of 1926, as he was feeling parched and fuzzled after battling with a particularly rebellious chapter, he thought he might take a month's holiday abroad. Clare having some business in London said she would join him a week or two later. When she eventually arrived at the German seaside resort which Sebastian had decided upon, she was unexpectedly informed at the hotel that he had left for an unknown destination but would be back in a couple of days. This puzzled Clare, although, as she afterwards told Miss Pratt, she did not feel unduly anxious or distressed. We may picture her, a thin tall figure in a blue mackintosh (the weather was overcast and unfriendly) strolling rather aimlessly on the promenade, the sandy beach, empty except for a few undismayed children, the three-coloured flags flapping mournfully in a dying breeze, and a steely gray sea breaking here and there into crests of foam. Farther down the coast there was a beech-wood, deep and dark with no undergrowth except bindwood patching the undulating brown soil; and a strange brown stillness stood waiting among the straight smooth tree-trunks: she thought she might find at any moment a red-capped German gnome peeping bright-eyed at her from among the dead leaves of a hollow. She unpacked her bathing things and passed a pleasant though somewhat listless day lying on the soft white sand. Next morning was rainy again and she stayed in her room until lunch time, reading Donne, who for ever after remained to her associated with the pale gray light of that damp and hazy day and the whine of a child wanting to play in the corridor. And presently Sebastian arrived. He was certainly glad to see her but there was something not quite natural in his demeanour. He seemed nervous and troubled, and averted his face whenever she tried to meet his look. He said he had come across a man he had known ages ago, in Russia, and they had gone in the man's car to—he named a place on the coast some miles away. "But what *is* the matter, my dear?" she asked peering into his sulky face.

"Oh, nothing, nothing," he cried peevishly, "I can't sit and do nothing, I want my work," he added and looked away.

"I wonder if you are telling me the truth," she said.

He shrugged his shoulders and slid the edge of his palm along the groove of the hat he was holding.

"Come along," he said, "Let's have lunch and then go back to London."

But there was no convenient train before evening. As the

weather had cleared they went out for a stroll. Sebastian tried once or twice to be as bright with her as he usually was, but it somehow fizzled out and they were both silent. They reached the beechwood. There was the same mysterious and dull suspense about it, and he said, though she had not told him she had been there before: "What a funny quiet place. Eerie, isn't it? One half-expects to see a brownie among those dead leaves and convolvulus."

"Look here, Sebastian," she suddenly exclaimed, putting her hands on his shoulders. "I want to know what's the matter. Perhaps you've stopped loving me. Is it that?"

"Oh my darling, what nonsense," said he with perfect sincerity. "But . . . if you must know . . . you see . . . I'm not good at deceiving, and well, I'd rather you knew. The fact is I felt a confounded pain in my chest and arm, so I thought I'd better dash to Berlin and see a doctor. He packed me off to bed there . . . Serious? . . . No, I hope not. We discussed coronary arteries and blood supply and sinuses of Salva and he generally seemed to be a very knowing old beggar. I'll see another man in London and get a second opinion, though I feel fit as a fiddle to-day . . ."

I suppose Sebastian already knew from what exact heart-disease he was suffering. His mother had died of the same complaint, a rather rare variety of angina pectoris, called by some doctors "Lehmann's disease." It appears, however, that after the first attack he had at least a year's respite, though now and then he did experience a queer twinge as of inner itch in his left arm.

He sat down to his task again and worked steadily through the autumn, spring and winter. The composing of *Success* turned out to be even more arduous than that of his first novel and took him much longer, although both books were about the same length. By a stroke of luck I have a direct picture of the day *Success* was finished. This I owe to someone I met later—and indeed many of the impressions I have offered in this chapter have been formed by corroborating the statements of Miss Pratt with those of another friend of Sebastian's, though the spark which had kindled it all belongs in some mysterious manner to that glimpse I had of Clare Bishop walking heavily down a London street.

The door opens. Sebastian Knight is disclosed lying spread-eagled on the floor of his study. Clare is making a neat bundle of the typed sheets on the desk. The person who entered stops short.

"No, Leslie," says Sebastian from the floor, "I'm not dead. I have finished building a world, and this is my Sabbath rest."

"THE PRISMATIC BEZEL" was appreciated at its true worth only when Sebastian's first real success caused it to be presented anew by another firm (Bronson), but even then it did not sell as well as *Success*, or *Lost Property*. For a first novel it shows remarkable force of artistic will and literary self-control. As often was the way with Sebastian Knight he used parody as a kind of springboard for leaping into the highest region of serious emotion. J. L. Coleman has called it "a clown developing wings, an angel mimicking a tumbler pigeon," and the metaphor seems to me very apt. Based cunningly on a parody of certain tricks of the literary trade, *The Prismatic Bezel* soars skyward. With something akin to fanatical hate Sebastian Knight was ever hunting out the things which had once been fresh and bright but which were now worn to a thread, dead things among living ones; dead things shamming life, painted and repainted, continuing to be accepted by lazy minds serenely unaware of the fraud. The decayed idea might be in itself quite innocent and it may be argued that there is not much sin in continually exploiting this or that thoroughly worn subject or style if it still pleases and amuses. But for Sebastian Knight, the merest trifle, as, say, the adopted method of a detective story, became a bloated and malodorous corpse. He did not mind in the least "penny dreadfuls" because he wasn't concerned with ordinary morals; what annoyed him

91

invariably was the second rate, not the third or N-th rate, because here, at the readable stage, the shamming began, and this was, in an *artistic* sense, immoral. But *The Prismatic Bezel* is not only a rollicking parody of the setting of a detective tale; it is also a wicked imitation of many other things: as for instance a certain literary habit which Sebastian Knight, with his uncanny perception of secret decay, noticed in the modern novel, namely the fashionable trick of grouping a medley of people in a limited space (a hotel, an island, a street). Then also different kinds of styles are satirized in the course of the book as well as the problem of blending direct speech with narration and description which an elegant pen solves by finding as many variations of "he said" as may be found in the dictionary between "acceded" and "yelped." But all this obscure fun is, I repeat, only the author's springboard.

Twelve persons are staying at a boarding-house; the house is very carefully depicted but in order to stress the "island" note, the rest of the town is casually shown as a secondary cross between natural mist and a primary cross between stage-properties and a real-estate agent's nightmare. As the author points out (indirectly) this method is somewhat allied to the cinema practice of showing the leading lady in her impossible dormitory years as glamorously different from a crowd of plain and fairly realistic schoolmates. One of the lodgers, a certain G. Abeson, art-dealer, is found murdered in his room. The local police-officer, who is described solely in terms of boots, rings up a London detective, asking him to come at once. Owing to a combination of mishaps (his car runs over an old woman and then he takes the wrong train) he is very long in arriving. In the meantime the inhabitants of the boarding house plus a chance passer-by, old Nosebag, who happened to be in the lobby when the crime was discovered, are thoroughly examined. All of them except the last named, a mild old gentleman with a white beard yellowish about the mouth, and a harmless passion for collecting snuffboxes, are more or less open to suspicion; and one of them, a fishy art-student, seems particularly so: half a dozen blood-stained handkerchiefs are found under his bed. Incidentally, it may be noted that in order to simplify and "concentrate" things not a single servant or hotel employee is specifically mentioned and nobody bothers about their non-existence. Then, with a quick sliding motion, something in the story begins to shift (the detective, it must be remembered, is still on the way and G. Abeson's stiff corpse lying on the carpet). It gradually transpires that all the lodgers are in various ways connected with one another. The old lady in No. 3 turns out to be the mother of the violinist in No. 11. The novelist occupying the front bedroom is really the husband of the young lady in the third floor back. The fishy art-student is no less than this lady's brother. The solemn moon-faced person who is so very polite to everyone, happens to be butler to the crusty old colonel who, it appears, is the violinist's father. The gradual melting process continues through the art-student's being engaged to the fat little woman in No. 5, and she is the old lady's daughter by a previous marriage. And when the amateur lawn tennis champion in No. 6 turns out to be the violinist's brother and the novelist their uncle and the old lady in No. 3 the crusty old colonel's wife, then the numbers on the doors are quietly wiped out and the boarding-house motif is painlessly and smoothly replaced by that of a country-house, with all its natural implications.

And here the tale takes on a strange beauty. The idea of time, which was made to look comic (detective losing his way . . . stranded somewhere in the night) now seems to curl up and fall asleep. Now the lives of the characters shine forth with a real and human significance and G. Abeson's sealed door is but that of a forgotten lumber-room. A new plot, a new drama utterly unconnected with the opening of the story, which is thus thrust back into the region of dreams, seems to struggle for existence and break into light. But at the very moment when the reader feels quite safe in an atmosphere of pleasurable reality and the grace and glory of the author's prose seems to indicate some lofty and rich intention, there is a grotesque knocking at the door and the detective enters. We are again wallowing in a morass of parody. The detective, a shifty fellow, drops his h's, and this is meant to look as if it were meant to look quaint; for it is not a parody of the Sherlock Holmes vogue but a parody of the modern reaction from it. The lodgers are examined afresh. New clues are guessed at. Mild old Nosebag potters about, very absent-minded and harmless. He had just dropped in to see if they had a spare room, he explains. The old gag of making the most innocent-looking person turn out to be the master-villain seems to be on the point of being exploited. The sleuth suddenly gets interested in snuffboxes. " 'Ullo," he says, " 'ow about Hart?" Suddenly a policeman lumbers in, very red in the face and reports that the corpse has gone. The detective: "What dy'a mean by gorn?" The policeman: "Gone Sir, the room is empty." There was a moment of ridiculous suspense. "I think," said old Nosebag quietly, "that I can explain." Slowly and very carefully he removes his beard, his gray wig, his dark spectacles, and the face of G. Abeson is disclosed. "You see," says Mr. Abeson with a self-deprecating smile, "one dislikes being murdered."

I have tried my best to show the workings of the book, at least some of its workings. Its charm, humour and pathos can only be appreciated by direct reading. But for enlightenment of those who felt baffled by its habit of metamorphosis, or merely disgusted at finding something incompatible with the idea of a "nice book" in the discovery of a book's being an utterly new one, I should like to point out that *The Prismatic Bezel* can be thoroughly enjoyed once it is understood that the heroes of the book are what can be loosely called "methods of composition." It is as if a painter said: look, here I'm going to show you not the painting of a landscape, but the painting of different ways of painting a certain landscape, and I trust their harmonious fusion will disclose the landscape as I intend you to see it. In the first book Sebastian brought this experiment to a logical and satisfactory conclusion. By putting to the *ad absurdum* test this or that literary manner and then dismissing them one after the other, he deduced his own manner and fully exploited it in his next book *Success*. Here he seems to have passed from one plane to another rising a step higher, for, if his first novel is based on methods of literary composition,—the second one deals mainly with the methods of human fate. With scientific precision in the classification, examination and rejection of an immense amount of data (the accumulation of which is rendered possible by the fundamental assumption that an author is able to discover anything he may want to know about his characters, such capacity being limited only by the manner and purpose of his selection in so far as it ought to be not a haphazard jumble of worthless details but a definite and methodical quest), Sebastian Knight devotes the three hundred pages of *Success* to one of the most complicated researches that has ever been attempted by a writer. We are informed that a certain commercial traveller Percival Q. at a certain stage of his life and in certain circumstances meets the girl, a conjuror's assistant, with whom he will be happy ever after. The meeting is or seems accidental: both happen to use the same car belonging to an amiable stranger on a day the buses went on strike. This is the formula: quite uninteresting if viewed as an actual happening, but becoming a source of remarkable mental enjoyment and excitement, when examined from a special angle. The author's task is to find out how this formula has been arrived at; and all the magic and force of his art are summoned in order to discover the exact way in which two lines of life were made to come into contact,—the whole book indeed being but a glorious gamble on causalities or, if you prefer, the probing of the aetiological secret of aleatory occurrences. The odds seem unlimited. Several obvious lines of inquiry are followed with varying success. Working backwards the author finds out why the strike was fixed to take place that particular day and a certain politician's life-long predilection for the number nine is found to be at the root of the business. This leads us nowhere and the trail is abandoned (not without having given us the opportunity of witnessing a heated party debate). Another false scent is the stranger's car. We try to find out who he was and what caused him to pass at a given moment along a given street; but when we do learn that he had passed there on his way to his office every week day at the same time for the last ten years of his life, we are left none the wiser. Thus we are forced to assume that the outward circumstances of the meeting are not samples of fate's activity in regard to two subjects but a given entity, a fixed point, of no causal import; and so, with a clear conscience we turn to the problem of why Q. and the girl Anne of all people were made to come and stand side by side for a minute on the curb at that particular spot. So the girl's line of fate is traced back for a time, then the man's, notes are compared, and then again both lives are followed up in turn.

We learn a number of curious things. The two lines which have finally tapered to the point of meeting are really not the straight lines of a triangle which diverge steadily towards an unknown base, but wavy lines, now running wide apart, now almost touching. In other words there have been at least two occasions in these two peoples' lives when unknowingly to one another they all but met. In each case fate seemed to have prepared such a meeting with the utmost care; touching up now this possibility now that one; screening exits and re-painting signposts; narrowing in its creeping grasp the bag of the net where the butterflies were flapping; timing the least detail and leaving nothing to chance. The disclosure of these secret preparations is a fascinating one and the author seems argus-eyed as he takes into account all the colours of place and circumstance. But, every time, a minute mistake (the shadow of a flaw, the stopped hole of an unwatched possibility, a caprice of free will) spoils the necessitarian's pleasure and the two lives are diverging again with increased rapidity. Thus, Percival Q. is prevented, by a bee stinging him on the lip, at the last minute, from coming to the party, to which fate with endless difficulty had managed to bring Anne; thus, by a trick of temper she fails to get the carefully prepared job in the lost property office where Q.'s brother is employed.

But fate is much too persevering to be put off by failure. And when finally success is achieved it is reached by such delicate machinations that not the merest click is audible when at last the two are brought together.

I shall not go into further details of this clever and delightful novel. It is the best-known of Sebastian Knight's works, although his three later books surpass it in many ways. As in my demonstration of *The Prismatic Bezel*, my sole object is to show the workings, perhaps detrimentally to the impression of beauty left by the book itself, apart from its artifices. It contains, let me add, a passage so strangely connected with Sebastian's inner life at the time of the completing of the last chapters, that it deserves being quoted in contrast to a series of observations referring rather to the meanders of the author's brain than to the emotional side of his art.

"William [Anne's first queer effeminate fiancé, who afterwards jilted her] saw her home as usual and cuddled her a little in the darkness of the doorway. All of a sudden, she felt that his face was wet. He covered it with his hand and groped for his handkerchief. 'Raining in Paradise,' he said . . . 'the onion of happiness . . . poor Willy is willy nilly a willow.' He kissed the corner of her mouth and then blew his nose with a faint moist squizzle. 'Grown-up men don't cry,' said Anne. 'But I'm not a grown-up,' he replied with a whimper. 'That moon is childish, and that wet pavement is childish, and Love is a honey-suckling babe . . .' 'Please stop,' she said. 'You know I hate when you go on talking like that. It's so silly, so . . .' 'So Willy,' he sighed. He kissed her again and they stood like some soft dark statue with two dim heads. A policeman passed leading the night on a leash and then paused to let it sniff at a pillar-box. 'I'm as happy as you,' she said, 'but I don't want to cry in the least or to talk non-sense.' 'But can't you see,' he whispered, 'can't you see that happiness at its very best is but the zany of its own mortality?' 'Good-night,' said Anne. 'To-morrow at eight,' he cried as she slipped away. He patted the door gently and presently was strolling down the street. She is warm and she is pretty, he mused, and I love her, and it's all no good, no good, because we are dying. I cannot bear that backward glide into the past. That last kiss is already dead and *The Woman in White* [a film they had been to see that night] is stone-dead, and the policeman who passed is dead too, and even the door is as dead as its nail. And that last thought is already a dead thing by now. Coates (the doctor) is right when he says that my heart is too small for my size. And sighs. He wandered on talking to himself, his shadow now pulling a long nose, now dropping a curtsey, as it slipped back round a lamp-post. When he reached his dismal lodgings he was a long time climbing the dark stairs. Before going to bed he knocked at the conjuror's door and found the old man standing in his underwear and inspecting a pair of black trousers. 'Well?' said William . . . 'They don't kinda like my accent,' he re-plied, 'but I guess I'm going to get that turn all the same.' William sat down on the bed and said: 'You ought to dye your hair.' 'I'm more bald than gray,' said the conjuror. 'I sometimes wonder,' said William, 'where the things we shed are—because they must go *somewhere*, you know,—lost hair, fingernails . . .' 'Been drinking again,' suggested the con-juror without much curiosity. He folded his trousers with care and told William to quit the bed, so that he might put them under the mattress. William sat down on a chair and the conjuror went on with his business; the hairs bristled on his calves, his lips were pursed, his soft hands moved tenderly. 'I am merely happy,' said William. 'You don't look it,' said the solemn old man. 'May I buy you a rabbit?' asked William. 'I'll hire one when necessary,' the conjuror replied drawing out the 'necessary' as if it were an endless ribbon. 'A ridiculous profession,' said William, 'a pick-pocket gone mad, a matter of patter. The pennies in a beggar's cap and the omelette in your top hat. Absurdly the same.' 'We are used to insult,' said the conjuror. He calmly put out the light and William groped his way out. The books on the bed in his room seemed reluctant to move. As he undressed he imagined the forbidden bliss of a sunlit laundry: blue water and scarlet wrists. Might he beg Anne to wash his shirt? Had he really annoyed her again? Did she really believe they would be married some day? The pale little freckles on the glistening skin under her innocent eyes. The right front-tooth that protruded a little. Her soft warm neck. He felt again the pressure of tears. Would she go the way of May, Judy, Juliette, Augusta and all the rest of his love-embers? He heard the dancing-girl in the next room locking the door, washing, bumping down a jug, wistfully clearing her throat. Something dropped with a tinkle. The conjuror began to snore."

THE REAL LIFE OF SEBASTIAN KNIGHT

I AM fast approaching the crucial point of Sebastian's sentimental life and as I consider the work already done in the pale light of the task still before me I feel singularly ill at ease. Have I given as fair an idea of Sebastian's life up to now as I had hoped, and as I now hope to do, in regard to its final period? The dreary tussle with a foreign idiom and a complete lack of literary experience do not predispose one to feeling overconfident. But badly as I may have blundered over my task in the course of the preceding chapters I am determined to persevere and in this I am sustained by the secret knowledge that in some unobtrusive way Sebastian's shade is trying to be helpful.

I have received less abstract help too. P. G. Sheldon, the poet, who saw a great deal of Clare and Sebastian between 1927 and 1930 was kindly willing to tell me anything he might know, when I called upon him very soon after my strange half-meeting with Clare. And it is he again who a couple of months later (when I had already begun upon this book) informed me of poor Clare's fate. She had seemed to be such a normal and healthy young woman, how was it that she bled to death next to an empty cradle? He told me of her delight when *Success* lived up to its title. For it *was* a success this time. Why it is so, why this excellent book should flop and that other, as excellent, receive its due, will always remain something of a mystery. As had been the case, too, with his first novel, Sebastian had not moved a finger, not pulled the least string in order to have *Success* brightly heralded and warmly acclaimed. When a press-cutting agency began to pepper him with samples of praise, he refused either to subscribe to the clippings or thank the kindly critics. To express his gratitude to a man who by saying what he thought of a book was merely doing his duty, seemed to Sebastian improper and even insulting as implying a tepidly human side to the frosty serenity of dispassionate judgement. Moreover, once having begun he would have been forced to go on thanking and thanking for every following line lest the man should be hurt by a sudden lapse; and finally, such a damp dizzy warmth would develop that, in spite of this or that critic's well-known honesty, the grateful author might never be quite, quite certain that here or there personal sympathy had not tiptoed in.

Fame in our day is too common to be confused with the enduring glow around a deserving book. But whatever it was, Clare meant to enjoy it. She wanted to see people who wanted to see Sebastian, who emphatically did not want to see them. She wanted to hear strangers talk about *Success* but Sebastian said he was no longer interested in that particular book. She wanted Sebastian to join a literary club and mix with other authors. And once or twice Sebastian got into a starched shirt and got out of it again without having uttered one single word at the dinner arranged in his honour. He was not feeling too well. He slept badly. He had dreadful fits of temper—and this was a thing new to Clare. One afternoon as he was working at *The Funny Mountain* in his study and trying to keep to a steep slippery track among the dark crags of neuralgia, Clare entered and in her gentlest voice inquired whether he would not mind seeing a visitor.

"No," he said, baring his teeth at the word he had just written.

"But you asked him to come at five and . . ."

"Now you've done it . . ." cried Sebastian, and dashed his fountain-pen at the shocked white wall. "Can't you let me work in peace," he shouted in such a crescendo that P. G. Sheldon who had been playing chess with Clare in the next room got up and closed the door leading to the hall, where a meek little man was waiting.

Now and then, a wild frolicsome mood came over him. One afternoon with Clare and a couple of friends, he devised a beautiful practical joke to be played on a person they were going to meet after dinner. Sheldon curiously enough had forgotten what it was exactly, that scheme. Sebastian laughed and turned on his heel knocking his fists together as he did when genuinely amused. They were all about to start and very eager and all that, and Clare had 'phoned for a taxi and her new silver shoes glittered and she had found her bag, when suddenly Sebastian seemed to lose all interest in the proceedings. He looked bored and yawned almost without opening his mouth in a very annoying manner and presently said he would take the dog out and then go to bed. In those days he had a little black bull-terrier; eventually it fell ill and had to be destroyed.

The *Funny Mountain* was completed, then *Albinos in Black* and then his third and last short story, *The Back of the Moon*. You remember that delightful character in it—the meek little man waiting for a train who helped three miserable travellers in three different ways? This Mr. Siller is perhaps the most alive of Sebastian's creatures and is incidentally the final representative of the "research theme," which I have discussed in conjunction with *The Prismatic Bezel* and *Success*. It is as though a certain idea steadily growing through two books has now burst into real physical existence, and so Mr. Siller makes his bow, with every detail of habit and manner, palpable and unique—: the bushy eyebrows and the modest mustache, the soft collar and the Adam's apple "moving like the bulging shape of an arrased eavesdropper," the brown eyes, the wine-red veins on the big strong nose, "whose form made one wonder whether he had not lost his hump somewhere"; the little black tie and the old umbrella ("a duck in deep mourning"); the dark thickets in the nostrils; the beautiful surprise of shiny perfection when he removes his hat. But the better Sebastian's work was the worse he felt—especially in the intervals. Sheldon thinks that the world of the last book he was to write several years later (*The Doubtful Asphodel*) was already casting its shadow on all things surrounding him and that his novels and stories were but bright masks, sly tempters under the pretense of artistic adventure leading him unerringly towards a certain imminent goal. He was presumably as fond of Clare as he had always been, but the acute sense of mortality which had begun to obsess him, made his relations with her appear more brittle than they perhaps were. As for Clare, she had quite inadvertently in her well-meaning innocence dallied at some pleasant sunlit corner of Sebastian's life, where Sebastian himself had not paused; and now she was left behind and did not quite know whether to try and catch up with him or attempt to call him back. She was kept cheerfully busy, what with looking after Sebastian's literary affairs and keeping his life tidy in general, and although she surely felt that something was awry, that it was dangerous to lose touch with his imaginative existence, she probably comforted herself by presuming it to be a passing restlessness, and that "it would all settle down by-and-by." Naturally, I cannot touch upon the intimate side of their relationship, firstly, because it would be ridiculous to discuss what no one can definitely assert, and secondly because the very sound of the word "sex" with its hissing vulgarity and the "ks, ks" catcall at the end, seems so inane to me that I cannot help doubting whether there *is* any real idea behind the word. Indeed, I believe that granting "sex" a special situation when tackling a human problem, or worse still, letting the "sexual idea," if such a thing exists, pervade and "explain" all the rest is a grave error of reasoning. "The breaking of a wave cannot explain the whole sea, from its moon to its serpent; but a pool in the cup of a rock and the diamond-rippled road to Cathay are both water." (*The Back of the Moon.*)

"Physical love is but another way of saying the same thing and not a special sexophone note, which once heard is echoed in every other region of the soul" (*Lost Property*, page 82). "All things belong to the same order of things, for such is the oneness of human perception, the oneness of individuality, the oneness of matter, whatever matter may be. The only real number is one, the rest are mere repetition" (*ibid*, page 83). Had I even known from some reliable source that Clare was not quite up to the standards of Sebastian's love-making I would still never dream of selecting this dissatisfaction as the reason for his general feverishness and nervousness. But being dissatisfied with things in general, he might have been dissatisfied with the colour of his romance too. And mind you, I use the word dissatisfaction very loosely, for Sebastian's mood at that period of his life was something far more complicated than mere Weltschmerz or the blues. It can only be grasped through the medium of his last book *The Doubtful Asphodel*. That book was as yet but a distant haze. Presently it would become the outline of a shore. In 1929, a famous heart-specialist, Dr. Oates, advised Sebastian to spend a month at Blauberg, in Alsace, where a certain treatment had proved beneficial in several similar cases. It seems to have been tacitly agreed that he would go alone. Before he left, Miss Pratt, Sheldon, Clare and Sebastian had tea together at his flat and he was cheerful and talkative, and teased Clare for having dropped her own crumpled handkerchief among the things she had been packing for him in his fussy presence. Then he made a dart at Sheldon's cuff (he never wore a wristwatch himself), peeped at the time and suddenly began to rush, although there was almost an hour to spare. Clare did not suggest seeing him to the train—she knew he disliked that. He kissed her on the temple and Sheldon helped him carry out his bag (have I already mentioned that, apart from a vague charwoman and the waiter who brought him his meals from a neighbouring restaurant, Sebastian did not employ servants?). When he had gone, the three of them sat in silence for a while.

All at once Clare put down the teapot and said: "I think that handkerchief had wanted to go with him, I've a great mind to take that hint."

"Don't be silly," said Mr. Sheldon.

"Why not?" she asked.

"If you mean that you want to catch the same train," began Miss Pratt . . .

"Why not," Clare repeated. "I have forty minutes in which to do it. I'll dash to my place, pack a thing or two, bolt into a taxi . . ."

And she did it. What happened at Victoria is not known, but an hour or so later she rang up Sheldon who had gone home, and told him with a rather pathetic little laugh that Sebastian had not even wanted her to stay on the platform until his train left. I have a very definite vision somehow of her arriving there, with her bag, her lips ready to part in a humorous smile, her dim eyes peering through the windows of the train, looking for him, then finding him, or perhaps he saw her first . . . "Hullo, here I am," she must have said brightly, a little too brightly perhaps . . .

He wrote to her, a few days later, to tell her that the place was very pleasant and that he felt remarkably well. Then there was a silence, and only when Clare had sent an anxious telegram did a card arrive with the information that he was curtailing his stay at Blauberg and would spend a week in Paris before coming home.

Towards the end of that week he rang me up and we dined together at a Russian restaurant. I had not seen him since 1924 and this was 1929. He looked worn and ill, and owing to his pallor seemed unshaven although he had just been to the barber. There was a boil at the back of his neck patched up with pink plaster.

After he had asked me a few questions about myself, we both found it a strain to carry on the conversation. I asked him what had become of the nice girl with whom I had seen him last time. "What girl?" he asked. "Oh, Clare. Yes, she's all right. We're sort of married."

"You look a bit seedy," I said.

"And I don't give a damn if I do. Will you have 'pelmenies' now?"

"Fancy your still remembering what they taste like," I said.

"Why shouldn't I?" he said drily.

We ate in silence for some minutes. Then we had coffee.

"What did you say the place was called? Blauberg?"

"Yes, Blauberg."

"Was it nice there?"

"It depends on what you call nice," he said and his jaw-muscles moved as he scrunched a yawn. "Sorry," he said, "I hope I get some sleep in the train."

He suddenly fumbled at my wrist.

"Half-past eight," I replied.

"I've got to telephone," he muttered and strode across the restaurant with his napkin in his hand. Five minutes later he was back with the napkin half-stuffed into his coat-pocket. I pulled it out.

"Look here," he said, "I'm dreadfully sorry, I must be going. I forgot I had an appointment."

"It has always distressed me," writes Sebastian Knight in *Lost Property* "that people in restaurants never notice the animated mysteries, who bring them their food and check their overcoats and push doors open for them. I once reminded a businessman with whom I had lunched a few weeks before, that the woman who had handed us our hats had had cotton wool in her ears. He looked puzzled and said he hadn't been aware of there having been any woman at all. . . . A person who fails to notice a taxi-driver's hare-lip because he is in a hurry to get somewhere, is to me a monomaniac. I have often felt as if I were sitting among blind men and mad-men, when I thought that I was the only one in the crowd to wonder about the chocolate-girl's slight, very slight limp."

As we left the restaurant and were making our way towards the taxi-rank, a bleary-eyed old man wetted his thumb and offered Sebastian or me or both, one of the printed advertisements he was distributing. Neither of us took it, both looked straight ahead, sullen dreamers ignoring the offer. "Well, good-bye," I said to Sebastian, as he beckoned to a cab.

"Come and see me one day in London," he said and glanced over his shoulder, "Wait a minute," he added, "this won't do. I have cut a beggar . . ." He left me and presently returned, a small sheet of paper in his hand. He read it carefully before throwing it away.

"Want a lift?" he asked.

I felt he was madly anxious to get rid of me.

"No, thanks," I said. I did not catch the address he gave to the chauffeur, but I recall his telling him to go fast.

When he returned to London . . . No, the thread of the narrative breaks off and I must ask others to tie up the threads again.

Did Clare notice at once that something had happened? Did she suspect at once what that something was? Shall we try to guess what she asked Sebastian, and what he answered, and what she said then? I think we will not . . . Sheldon saw them soon after Sebastian's return and found that Sebastian looked queer. But he had looked queer before, too . . .

"Presently it began to worry me," said Mr. Sheldon. He met Clare alone and asked her whether she thought Sebastian was all right. "Sebastian?" said Clare with a slow dreadful smile, "Sebastian has gone mad. Quite mad," she repeated, widely opening her pale eyes.

"He has stopped talking to me," she added in a small voice.

Then Sheldon saw Sebastian and asked him what was amiss.

"Is it any of your business?" inquired Sebastian with a kind of wretched coolness.

"I like Clare," said Sheldon, "and I want to know why she walks about like a lost soul." (She would come to Sebastian every day and sit in odd corners where she never used to sit. She brought sweets sometimes or a tie for Sebastian. The sweets remained uneaten and the tie hung lifelessly on the back of a chair. She seemed to pass through Sebastian like a ghost. Then she would fade away as silently as she had come).

"Well," said Sheldon, "out with it, man. What have you done to her?"

SHELDON learnt nothing from him whatsoever. What he did learn was from Clare herself; and this amounted to very little. After his return to London Sebastian had been getting letters in Russian from a woman he had met at Blauberg. She had been living at the same hotel as he. Nothing else was known.

Six weeks later (in September, 1929) Sebastian left England again and was absent until January of the following year. Nobody knew where he had been. Sheldon suggested it might have been Italy "because lovers usually go there." He did not cling to his suggestion.

Whether Sebastian had some final explanation with Clare, or whether he left a letter for her when he departed, is not clear. She wandered away as quietly as she had come. She changed her lodgings: they were too close to Sebastian's flat. On a certain gloomy November day Miss Pratt met her in the fog on her way home from a life-insurance office where she had found work. After that, the two girls saw each other fairly often, but Sebastian's name was seldom mentioned. Five years later, Clare married.

Lost Property which Sebastian had begun at that time appears as a kind of halt in his literary journey of discovery: a summing up, a counting of the things and souls lost on the way, a setting of bearings; the clinking sound of unsaddled horses browsing in the dark; the glow of a campfire; stars overhead. There is in it a short chapter dealing with an aeroplane crash (the pilot and all the passengers but one were killed); the survivor, an elderly Englishman, was discovered by a farmer some way from the place of the accident, sitting on a stone. He sat huddled up—the picture of misery and pain. "Are you badly hurt?" asked the farmer. "No," answered the Englishman, "toothache. I've had it all the way." Half a dozen letters were found scattered in a field: remnants of the air-mail bag. Two of these were business letters of great importance; a third was addressed to a woman, but began: "Dear Mr. Mortimer, in reply to yours of the 6th inst . . ." and dealt with the placing of an order; a fourth was a birthday greeting; a fifth was the letter of a spy with its steely secret hidden in a haystack of idle prattle; and the last was an envelope directed to a firm of traders with the wrong letter inside, a love letter. "This will smart, my poor love. Our picnic is finished; the dark road is bumpy and the smallest child in the car is about to be sick. A cheap fool would tell you: you must be brave. But then, anything I might tell you in the way of support or consolation is sure to be milk-puddingy,—you know what I mean. You always knew what I meant. Life with you was lovely—and when I say lovely, I mean doves and lilies, and velvet, and that soft pink 'v' in the middle and the way your tongue curved up to the long, lingering 'l.' Our life together was alliterative, and when I think of all the little things which will die, now that we cannot share them, I feel as if we were dead too. And perhaps we are. You see, the greater our happiness was, the hazier its edges grew, as if its outlines were melting, and now it has dissolved altogether. I have not stopped loving you; but something is dead in me, and I cannot see you in the mist . . . This is all poetry. I am lying to you. Lily-livered. There can be nothing more cowardly than a poet beating about the bush. I think you have guessed how things stand: the damned formula of 'another woman.' I am desperately unhappy with her—here is one thing which is true. And I think there is nothing much more to be said about that side of the business.

"I cannot help feeling there is something essentially wrong about love. Friends may quarrel or drift apart, close relations too, but there is not this pang, this pathos, this fatality which clings to love. Friendship never has that doomed look. Why, what is the matter? I have not stopped loving you, but because I cannot go on kissing your dim dear face, we must part, we must part. Why is it so? What is this mysterious exclusiveness? One may have a thousand friends, but only one love-mate. Harems have nothing to do with this matter: I am speaking of dance, not gymnastics. Or can one imagine a tremendous Turk loving every one of his four hundred wives as I love you? For if I say 'two' I have started to count and there is no end to it. There is only one real number: One. And love, apparently, is the best exponent of this singularity.

"Good-bye, my poor love. I shall never forget you and never replace you. It would be absurd of me to try and persuade you that you were the pure love, and that this other passion is but a comedy of the flesh. All is flesh and all is purity. But one thing is certain: I have been happy with you and now I am miserable with another. And so life will go on. I shall joke with the chaps at the office and enjoy my dinners (until I get dyspepsia), and read novels, and write verse, and keep an eye on the stocks—and generally behave as I have always behaved. But that does not mean that I shall be happy without you . . . Every small thing which will remind me of you—the look of disapproval about the furniture in the rooms where you have patted cushions and spoken to the poker, every small thing which we have descried together— will always seem to me one half of a shell, one half of a penny, with the other half kept by you. Good-bye. Go away, go away. Don't write. Marry Charlie or any other good man with a pipe in his teeth. Forget me now, but remember me afterwards, when the bitter part is forgotten. This blot is not due to a tear. My fountain-pen has broken down and I am using a filthy pen in this filthy hotel room. The heat is terrific and I have not been able to clinch the business I was supposed to bring 'to a satisfactory close,' as that ass Mortimer says. I think you have got a book or two of mine—but that is not really important. *Please*, don't write. L."

If we abstract from this fictitious letter everything that is personal to its supposed author, I believe that there is much in it that may have been felt by Sebastian, or even written by him, to Clare. He had a queer habit of endowing even his most grotesque characters with this or that idea, or impression, or desire which he himself might have toyed with. His hero's letter may possibly have been a kind of code in which he expressed a few truths about his relations with Clare. But I fail to name any other author who made use of his art in such a baffling manner—baffling to me who might desire to see the real man behind the author. The light of personal truth is hard to perceive in the shimmer of an imaginary nature, but what is still harder to understand is the amazing fact that a man writing of things which he really felt at the time of writing, could have had the power to create simultaneously—and out of the very things which distressed his mind—a fictitious and faintly absurd character.

Sebastian returned to London in the beginning of 1930 and took to his bed after a very bad heart attack. Somehow or other he managed to go on with the writing of *Lost Property*: his easiest book, I think. Now, it ought to be understood in connection with what follows that Clare had been solely responsible for the managing of his literary affairs. After her departure, these soon became wildly entangled. In many cases Sebastian had not the vaguest idea how things stood and what his exact relations with this or that publisher were. He was so muddled, so utterly incompetent, so hopelessly incapable of remembering a single name or address, or the place where he put things, that now he got into the most absurd predicaments. Curiously enough, Clare's girlish forgetfulness had been replaced by a perfect clarity and steadiness of purpose when handling Sebastian's affairs; but now it all went amuck. He had never learnt to use a typewriter and was much too nervous to begin now. *The Funny Mountain* was published simultaneously in two American magazines, and Sebastian was at a loss to remember how he had managed to sell it to two different people. Then there was a complicated affair with a man who wanted to make a film of *Success* and who had paid Sebastian in advance (without his noticing it, so absent-mindedly did he read letters) for a shortened and "intensified" version, which Sebastian never even dreamt of making. *The Prismatic Bezel* was in the market again, but Sebastian hardly knew of it. Invitations were not even answered. Telephone numbers proved delusions, and the harassing search for the envelope where he had scrawled this or that number exhausted him more than the writing of a chapter. And then—his mind was elsewhere, following in the tracks of an absent mistress, waiting for her call,—and presently the call would come, or he himself could stand the suspense no longer, and there he would be as Roy Carswell had once seen him: a gaunt man in a great coat and bedroom slippers getting into a Pullman car.

It was in the beginning of this period that Mr. Goodman made his appearance. Little by little, Sebastian handed over to him all his literary affairs, and felt greatly relieved to meet so efficient a secretary. "I usually found him," writes Mr. Goodman, "lying in bed like a sulky leopard" (which somehow reminds one of the nightcapped wolf in "Little Red Riding Hood") . . . "Never in my life had I seen," he goes on in another passage, "such a dejected-looking being . . . I am told that the French author M. Proust, whom Knight consciously or subconsciously copied, also had a great inclination towards a certain listless 'interesting' pose . . ." And further: "Knight was very thin, with a pale countenance and sensitive hands, which he liked to display with feminine coquetry. He confessed to me once that he liked to pour half a bottle of French perfume into his morning bath, but with all that he looked singularly badly got up . . . Knight was extraordinarily vain, like most modernist authors. Once or twice I caught him pasting cuttings, most certainly reviews concerning his books, into a beautiful and expensive album which he kept locked up in his desk, feeling perhaps a little ashamed to let my critical eye consider the fruit of his human weakness . . . He often went abroad, twice a year, I daresay, presumably to Gay Paree . . . But he was very mysterious about it and made a great show of Byronic langour. I cannot help feeling that trips to the Continent formed part of his artistic program . . . he was the perfect 'poseur.' "

But where Mr. Goodman waxes really eloquent is when

he starts to discourse upon deeper matters. His idea is to show and explain the "fatal split between Knight the artist and the great booming world about him"—(a circular fissure, obviously). "Knight's uncongeniality was his undoing," exclaims Goodman and clicks out three dots. "Aloofness is a cardinal sin in an age when a perplexed humanity eagerly turns to its writers and thinkers, and demands of them attention to, if not the cure of, its woes and wounds . . . The 'ivory tower' cannot be suffered unless it is transformed into a lighthouse or a broadcasting station . . . In such an age . . . brimming with burning problems when . . . economic depression . . . dumped . . . cheated . . . the man in the street . . . the growth of totalitarian . . . unemployment . . . the next super-great war . . . new aspects of family life . . . sex . . . structure of the universe." Mr. Goodman's interests are wide, as we see. "Now, Knight," he goes on, "absolutely refused to take any interest whatsoever in contemporary questions . . . When asked to join in this or that movement, to take part in some momentous meeting, or merely to append his signature, among more famous names, to some manifest of undying truth or denunciation of great iniquity . . . he flatly refused in spite of all my admonishments and even pleadings . . . True, in his last (and most obscure) book, he does survey the world . . . but the angle he chooses and the aspects he notes are totally different from what a serious reader naturally expects from a serious author . . . It is as though a conscientious inquirer into the life and machinery of some great enterprise were shown, with elaborate circumlocution, a dead bee on a window sill . . . Whenever I called his attention to this or that just published book which had fascinated me because it was of general and vital interest, he childishly re-

plied that it was 'claptrap,' or made some other completely
irrelevant remark . . . He confused solitude with altitude and
the Latin for sun. He failed to realise that it was merely a dark
corner . . . However, as he was hypersensitive (I remember
how he used to wince when I pulled my fingers to make the
joints crack,—a bad habit I have when meditating), he
could not help feeling that something was wrong . . . that he
was steadily cutting himself away from Life . . . and that the
switch would not function in his solarium. The misery which
had begun as an earnest young man's reaction to the rude
world into which his temperamental youth had been thrust,
and which later continued to be displayed as a fashionable
mask in the days of his success as a writer, now took on a
new and hideous reality. The board adorning his breast read
no more 'I am the lone artist'; invisible fingers had changed
it into 'I am blind.' "

It would be an insult to the reader's acumen were I to comment on Mr. Goodman's glibness. If Sebastian was blind, his
secretary, in any case, plunged lustily into the part of a bark-
ing and pulling leader. Roy Carswell, who in 1933 was
painting Sebastian's portrait, told me he remembered roaring with laughter at Sebastian's accounts of his relations with
Mr. Goodman. Very possibly he would never have been energetic enough to get rid of that pompous person had the latter
not become a shade too enterprising. In 1934 Sebastian wrote
to Roy Carswell from Cannes telling him that he had found
out by chance (he seldom reread his own books) that Goodman had changed an epithet in the Swan edition of *The
Funny Mountain*. "I have given him the sack," he added. Mr.
Goodman modestly refrains from mentioning this minor detail. After exhausting his stock of impressions, and conclud-

ing that the real cause of Sebastian's death was the final realisation of having been "a human failure, and therefore an artistic one too," he cheerfully mentions that his work as secretary came to an end owing to his entering another branch of business. I shall not refer any more to Goodman's book. It is abolished.

But as I look at the portrait Roy Carswell painted I seem to see a slight twinkle in Sebastian's eyes, for all the sadness of their expression. The painter has wonderfully rendered the moist dark greenish-grey of their iris, with a still darker rim and a suggestion of gold dust constellating round the pupil. The lids are heavy and perhaps a little inflamed, and a vein or two seems to have burst on the glossy eye-ball. These eyes and the face itself are painted in such a manner as to convey the impression that they are mirrored Narcissus-like in clear water—with a very slight ripple on the hollow cheek, owing to the presence of a water-spider which has just stopped and is floating backward. A withered leaf has settled on the reflected brow, which is creased as that of a man peering intently. The crumpled dark hair over it is partly suffused by another ripple, but one strand on the temple has caught a glint of humid sunshine. There is a deep furrow between the straight eyebrows, and another down from the nose to the tightly shut dusky lips. There is nothing much more than this head. A dark opalescent shade clouds the neck, as if the upper part of the body were receding. The general background is a mysterious blueness with a delicate trellis of twigs in one corner. Thus Sebastian peers into a pool at himself.

"I wanted to hint at a woman somewhere behind him or over him,—the shadow of a hand, perhaps . . . something . . .

But then I was afraid of story-telling instead of painting."

"Well, nobody seems to know anything about her. Not even Sheldon."

"She smashed his life, that sums her up, doesn't it?"

"No, I want to know more. I want to know all. Otherwise he will remain as incomplete as your picture. Oh, it is very good, the likeness is excellent, and I love that floating spider immensely. Especially its club-footed shadow at the bottom. But the face is only a chance reflection. Any man can look into water."

"But don't you think that he did it particularly well?"

"Yes, I can see your point. But all the same I must find that woman. She is the missing link in his evolution, and I must obtain her—it's a scientific necessity."

"I'll bet you this picture that you won't find her," said Roy Carswell.

THE REAL LIFE OF
SEBASTIAN KNIGHT

THE first thing was to learn her identity. How should I start upon my quest? What data did I possess? In June, 1929, Sebastian had dwelt at the Beaumont Hotel at Blauberg, and there he had met her. She was Russian. No other clue was available.

I have Sebastian's aversion for postal phenomena. It seems easier to me to travel a thousand miles than to write the shortest letter, then find an envelope, find the right address, buy the right stamp, post the letter (and rack my brain trying to remember whether I have signed it). Moreover, in the delicate affair I was about to tackle, correspondence was out of the question. In March, 1936, after a month's stay in England, I consulted a tourist office and set out for Blauberg.

So here he has passed, I reflected, as I looked at wet fields with long trails of white mist where upright poplar trees dimly floated. A small red-tiled town crouched at the foot of a soft grey mountain. I left my bag in the cloakroom of a forlorn little station where invisible cattle lowed sadly in some shunted truck, and went up a gentle slope towards a cluster of hotels and sanitariums beyond a damp-smelling park. There were very few people about, it was not "the height of the season," and I suddenly realised with a pang that I might find the hotel shut.

But it was not; thus far, luck was with me.

The house seemed fairly pleasant with its well kept garden

and budding chestnut trees. It looked as if it could not hold more than some fifty people—and this braced me: I wanted my choice restricted. The hotel manager was a grey-haired man with a trimmed beard and velvet black eyes. I proceeded very carefully.

First I said that my late brother, Sebastian Knight, a celebrated English author, had greatly liked his stay and that I was thinking of staying at the hotel myself in the summer. Perhaps I ought to have taken a room, sliding in, ingratiating myself, so to speak, and postponing my special request until a more favourable moment; but somehow I thought that the matter might be settled on the spot. He said yes, he remembered the Englishman who had stayed in 1929 and had wanted a bath every morning.

"He did not make friends readily, did he?" I asked with sham casualness. "He was always alone?"

"Oh, I think he was here with his father," said the hotel manager vaguely.

We wrestled for some time disentangling the three or four Englishmen who had happened to have stayed at Hotel Beaumont during the last ten years. I saw that he did not remember Sebastian any too clearly.

"Let me be frank," I said off-handedly, "I am trying to find the address of a lady, my brother's friend, who had stayed here at the same time as he."

The hotel manager lifted his eyebrows slightly, and I had the uneasy feeling that I had committed some blunder.

"Why?" he said. ("Ought I to bribe him?" I thought quickly.)

"Well," I said, "I'm ready to pay you for the trouble of finding the information I want."

"What information?" he asked. (He was a stupid and suspicious old party—may he never read these lines.)

"I was wondering," I went on patiently, "whether you would be so very, very kind as to help me to find the address of a lady who stayed here at the same time as Mr. Knight, that is in June, 1929?"

"What lady?" he asked in the elenctic tones of Lewis Carroll's caterpillar.

"I'm not sure of her name," I said nervously.

"Then how do you expect me to find her?" he said with a shrug.

"She was Russian," I said. "Perhaps you remember a Russian lady,—a *young* lady,—and well . . . good-looking?"

"*Nous avons eu beaucoup de jolies dames,*" he replied getting more and more distant. "How should I remember?"

"Well," said I, "the simplest way would be to have a look at your books and sort out the Russian names for June, 1929."

"There are sure to be several," he said. "How will you pick out the one you need, if you do not know it?"

"Give me the names and addresses," I said desperately, "and leave the rest to me."

He sighed deeply and shook his head.

"No," he said.

"Do you mean to say you don't keep books?" I asked trying to speak quietly.

"Oh, I keep them all right," he said. "My business requires great order in these matters. Oh, yes, I have got the names all right . . ."

He wandered away to the back of the room and produced a large black volume.

"Here," he said. "First week of July, 1935 . . . Professor Ott with wife, Colonel Samain . . ."

"Look here," I said, "I'm not interested in July, 1935. What I want . . " He shut his book and carried it away.

"I only wanted to show you," he said with his back turned to me,—"to show you [a lock clicked] that I keep my books in good order."

He came back to his desk and folded a letter that was lying on the blotting-pad.

"Summer, 1929," I pleaded. "Why don't you want to show me the pages I want?"

"Well," he said, "the thing is not done. Firstly, because I don't want a person who is a complete stranger to me to bother people who were and will be my clients. Secondly, because I cannot understand why you should be so eager to find a woman whom you do not want to name. And thirdly— I do not want to get into any kind of trouble. I have enough troubles as it is. In the hotel round the corner a Swiss couple committed suicide in 1929," he added rather irrelevantly.

"Is that your last word?" I asked.

He nodded and looked at his watch. I turned on my heel and slammed the door after me,—at least, I tried to slam it,— it was one of those confounded pneumatic doors which resist.

Slowly, I went back to the station. The park. Perhaps Sebastian recalled that particular stone bench under that cedar tree at the time he was dying. The outline of that mountain yonder may have been the paraph of a certain unforgettable evening. The whole place seemed to me a huge refuse heap where I knew a dark jewel had been lost. My failure was absurd, horrible, excruciating. The leaden sluggishness of dream-endeavour. Hopeless gropings among dissolving things. Why was the past so rebellious?

"And what shall I do now?" The stream of the biography on which I longed so to start, was, at one of its last bends, enshrouded in pale mist; like the valley I was contemplating. Could I leave it thus and write the book all the same? A book with a blind spot. An unfinished picture,—uncoloured limbs of the martyr with the arrows in his side.

I had the feeling that I was lost, that I had nowhere to go. I had pondered long enough the means to find Sebastian's last love to know that there was practically no other way of finding her name. Her name! I felt I should recognise it at once if I got at those greasy black folios. Ought I to give it up and turn to the collection of a few other minor details concerning Sebastian which I still needed and which I knew where to obtain?

It was in this bewildered state of mind that I got into the slow local train which was to take me back to Strasbourg. Then I would go on to Switzerland perhaps . . . But no, I could not get over the tingling pain of my failure; though I tried hard enough to bury myself in an English paper I had with me: I was in training, so to speak, reading only English in view of the work I was about to begin . . . But could one begin something so incomplete in one's mind?

I was alone in my compartment (as one usually is in a second-class carriage on that sort of train), but then, at the next station, a little man with bushy eyebrows got in, greeted me continentally, in thick guttural French, and sat down opposite. The train ran on, right into the sunset. All of a sudden, I noticed that the passenger opposite was beaming at me.

"Marrvellous weather," he said and took off his bowler hat disclosing a pink bald head. "You are English?" he asked nodding and smiling.

"Well, yes, for the moment," I answered.

"I see, saw, you read English djornal," he said pointing with his finger,—then hurriedly taking off his fawn glove and pointing again (perhaps he had been told that it was rude to point with a gloved index). I murmured something and looked away: I do not like chatting in a train, and at the moment I was particularly disinclined to do so. He followed my gaze. The low sun had set aflame the numerous windows of a large building which turned slowly, demonstrating one huge chimney, then another, as the train clattered by.

"Dat," said the little man," is 'Flambaum and Roth,' great fabric, factory. Paper."

There was a little pause. Then he scratched his big shiny nose and leaned towards me.

"I have been," he said, "London, Manchester, Sheffield, Newcastle." He looked at the thumb which had been left uncounted.

"Yes," he said. "De toy-business. Before de war. And I was playing a little football," he added, perhaps because he noticed that I glanced at a rough field with two goals dejectedly standing at the ends,—one of the two had lost its crossbar.

He winked; his small moustache bristled.

"Once, you know," he said and was convulsed with silent laughter, "once, you know, I fling, flung de ball from 'out' direct into goal."

"Oh," I said wearily, "and did you score?"

"De wind scored. Dat was a robinsonnada!"

"A what?"

"A robinsonnada—a marrvellous trick. Yes . . . Are you voyaging farr?" he inquired in a coaxing super-polite voice.

"Well," I said, "this train does not go farther than Strasbourg, does it?"

"No; I mean, meant in generahl. You are a traveller?"

I said yes.

"In what?" he asked, cocking his head.

"Oh, in the past I suppose," I replied.

He nodded as if he had understood. Then, leaning again towards me, he touched me on the knee and said: "Now I sell ledder—you know—ledder balls, for odders to play. Old! No force! Also hound-muzzles and fings like dat."

Again he tapped my knee lightly, "But earlier," he said, "last year, four last years, I was in de police—no, no, not once, not quite . . . Plain-clotheses. Understand me?"

I looked at him with sudden interest.

"Let me see," I said, "this gives me an idea . . ."

"Yes," he said, "if you want help, good ledder, *cigarette-etuis*, straps, advice, boxing-gloves . . ."

"Tifth and perhaps first," I said.

He took his bowler which lay on the seat near him, put it on carefully (his Adam's apple rolling up and down), and then, with a shiny smile, briskly took it off to me.

"My name is Silbermann," he said, and stretched out his hand. I shook it and named myself too.

"But dat is not English," he cried slapping his knee. "Dat is Russian! *Gavrit parussky?* I know also some odder words . . . Wait! Yes! Cookolkah—de little doll."

He was silent for a minute. I rolled in my head the idea he had given me. Should I try to consult a private detective agency? Would this little man be of any use himself?

"*Rebah!*" he cried. "Der's anodder. Fish, so? and . . . Yes. *Braht, millee braht*—dear brodder."

"I was thinking," I said, "that perhaps, if I told you of the bad fix I am in . . ."

"But dat is all," he said with a sigh. "I speak (again the fingers were counted) Lithuanian, German, English, French (and again the thumb remained). Forgotten Russian. Once! Quite!"

"Could you perhaps . . ." I began.

"Anyfing," he said. "Ledder-belts, purses, notice-books, suggestions."

"Suggestions," I said. "You see, I am trying to trace a person . . . a Russian lady whom I never have met, and whose name I do not know. All I know is that she lived for a certain stretch of time at a certain hotel at Blauberg."

"Ah, good place," said Mr. Silbermann, "very good"—and he screwed down the ends of his lips in grave approbation. "Good water, walks, caseeno. What you want me to do?"

"Well," I said, "I should first like to know what *can* be done in such cases."

"Better leave her alone," said Mr. Silbermann, promptly.

Then he thrust his head forward and his bushy eyebrows moved.

"Forget her," he said. "Fling her out of your head. It is dangerous and ewsyless." He flicked something off my trouser knee, nodded and sat back again.

"Never mind that," I said. "The question is how, not why."

"Every how has its why," said Mr. Silbermann. "You find, found her build, her picture, and now want to find herself yourself? Dat is not love. Ppah! Surface!"

"Oh, no," I cried, "it is not like that. I haven't the vaguest idea what she is like. But, you see, my dead brother loved her, and I want to hear her talk about him. It's really quite simple."

"Sad!" said Mr. Silbermann and shook his head.

"I want to write a book about him," I continued, "and every detail of his life interests me."

"What was he ill?" Mr. Silbermann asked huskily.

"Heart," I replied.

"Harrt,—dat's bad. Too many warnings, too many . . . general . . . general . . ."

"Dress rehearsals of death. That's right."

"Yes. And how old?"

"Thirty-six. He wrote books, under his mother's name. Knight. Sebastian Knight."

"Write it here," said Mr. Silbermann handing me an extraordinarily nice new note-book enclosing a delightful silver pencil. With a trk-trk-trk sound, he neatly removed the page, put it into his pocket and handed me the book again.

"You like it, no?" he said with an anxious smile. "Permit me a little present."

"Really," I said, "that's very kind . . ."

"Nofing, nofing," he said, waving his hand. "Now, what you want?"

"I want," I replied, "to get a complete list of all the people who have stayed in the Hotel Beaumont during June, 1929. I also want some particulars of who they are, the women at least. I want their addresses. I want to be sure that under a foreign name a Russian woman is not hidden. Then I shall choose the most probable one or ones and . . ."

"And try to reach dem," said Mr. Silbermann nodding. "Well! Very well! I had, have all the hotel-gentlemans here [he showed his palm], and it will be simple. Your address, please."

He produced another note-book, this time a very worn one, with some of the bescribbled pages falling off like autumn-leaves. I added that I should not move from Strasbourg until he called.

"Friday," he said. "Six, punctly."

Then the extraordinary little man sank back in his seat, folded his arms and closed his eyes, as if clinched business had somehow put a full stop to our conversation. A fly inspected his bald brow, but he did not move. He dozed until Strasbourg. There we parted.

"Look here," I said as we shook hands. "You must tell me your fee . . . I mean, I'm ready to pay you whatever you think suitable . . . And perhaps you would like something in advance . . ."

"You will send me your book," he said lifting a stumpy finger. And pay for possible depences," he added under his breath. "Cerrtainly!"

SO THIS was the way I got a list of some forty-two names among which Sebastian's (S. Knight, 36 Oak Park Gdns., London S.W.) seemed strangely lovely and lost. I was rather struck (pleasantly) by the fact that all the addresses were there too, affixed to the names: Silbermann hurriedly explained that people often die in Blauberg. Out of forty-one unknown persons as many as thirty-seven "did not come to question" as the little man put it. True, three of these (unmarried women) bore Russian names, but two of them were German and one Alsatian: they had often stayed at the hotel. There was also a somewhat baffling girl, Vera Rasine; Silbermann however knew for certain that she was French; that, in fact, she was a dancer and the mistress of a Strasbourg banker. There was also an aged Polish couple whom we let pass without a qualm. All the rest of this "out-of-the-question" group, that is thirty one persons, consisted of twenty adult males; of these only eight were married or at least had brought their wives (Emma, Hildegard, Pauline and so on), all of whom Silbermann swore were elderly, respectable and eminently non-Russian.

Thus we were left with four names:

Mademoiselle Lidya Bohemsky with an address in Paris. She had spent nine days in the hotel at the beginning of Sebastian's stay and the manager did not remember anything about her.

Madame de Rechnoy. She had left the hotel for Paris on the eve of Sebastian's departure for the same city. The manager remembered that she was a smart young woman and very generous with her tips. The "de" denoted, I knew, a certain type of Russian who likes to accent gentility, though really the use of the French *particule* before a Russian name is not only absurd but illegal. She might have been an adventuress; she might have been the wife of a snob.

Helene Grinstein. The name was Jewish but in spite of the "stein" it was not German-Jewish. That "i" in "grin" displacing the natural "u" pointed to its having grown in Russia. She had arrived but a week before Sebastian left and had stayed three days longer. The manager said she was a pretty woman. She had been to his hotel once before and lived in Berlin.

Helene von Graun. That was a real German name. But the manager was positive that several times during her stay she had sung songs in Russian. She had a splendid contralto, he said, and was ravishing. She had remained a month in all, leaving for Paris five days before Sebastian.

I meticulously noted all these particulars and the four addresses. Any of these four might prove to be the one I wanted. I warmly thanked Mr. Silbermann as he sat there before me with his hat on his joined knees. He sighed and looked down at the toes of his small black boots adorned by old mouse-grey spats.

"I have made dis," he said, "because you are to me sympathetic. But . . . [he looked at me with mild appeal in his bright brown eyes] but please, I fink it is ewsyless. You can't see de odder side of de moon. Please donnt search de woman. What is past is past. She donnt remember your brodder."

"I shall jolly well remind her," I said grimly.

"As you desire," he muttered squaring his shoulders and buttoning up his coat. He got up. "Good djorney," he said without his usual smile.

"Oh, wait a bit, Mr. Silbermann, we've got to settle something. What do I owe you?"

"Yes, dat is correct," he said seating himself again. "Moment." He unscrewed his fountain pen, jotted down a few figures, looked at them tapping his teeth with the holder: "Yes, sixty-eight francs."

"Well, that's not much," I said, "won't you perhaps . . ."

"Wait," he cried, "dat is false. I have forgotten . . . do you guard dat notice-book dat I give, gave you?"

"Why, yes," I said, "in fact, I've begun using it. You see . . . I thought . . ."

"Den it is not sixty-eight," he said, rapidly revising his addition. "It is . . . It is only eighteen, because de book costs fifty. Eighteen francs in all. Travelling depences . . ."

"But," I said, rather flabbergasted at his arithmetic . . .

"No, dat's now right," said Mr. Silbermann.

I found a twenty franc coin though I would have gladly given him a hundred times as much, if he had only let me.

"So," he said, "I owe you now . . . Yes, dat's right, Eighteen and two make twenty." He knitted his brows. "Yes, twenty. Dat's yours." He put my coin on the table and was gone.

I wonder how I shall send him this work when it is finished: the funny little man has not given me his address, my head was too full of other things to think of asking him for it. But if he ever does come across *The Real Life of Sebastian Knight* I should like him to know how grateful I am for his help. And for the note-book. It is well filled by now, and I shall have a new set of pages clipped in when these are completed.

After Mr. Silbermann had gone I studied at length the four addresses he had so magically obtained for me, and I decided to begin with the Berlin one. If that proved a disappointment I should be able to grapple with a trio of possibilities in Paris without undertaking another long journey, a journey all the more enervating because then I should know for sure I was playing my very last card. If on the contrary, my first try was lucky, then . . . But no matter . . . Fate amply rewarded me for my decision.

Large wet snowflakes were drifting aslant the Passauer Strasse in West-Berlin as I approached an ugly old house, its face half-hidden in a mask of scaffolding. I tapped on the glass of the porter's lodge, a muslin curtain was roughly drawn aside, a small window was knocked open and a blowsy old woman gruffly informed me that Frau Helene Grinstein did live in the house. I felt a queer little shiver of elation and went up the stairs. "Grinstein," said a brass plate on the door.

A silent boy in a black tie with a pale swollen face let me in and without so much as asking my name, turned and walked down the passage. There was a crowd of coats on the rack in the tiny hall. A bunch of snow-wet chrysanthemums lay on the table between two solemn top hats. As no one seemed to come, I knocked at one of the doors, then pushed it open and then shut it again. I had caught a glimpse of a dark-haired little girl, lying fast asleep on a divan, under a moleskin coat. I stood for a minute in the middle of the hall. I wiped my face which was still wet from snow. I blew my nose. Then I ventured down the passage. A door was ajar and I caught the sound of low voices, speaking in Russian. There were many people in the two large rooms joined by a kind of arch. One or two faces turned towards me vaguely as I strolled in, but otherwise my entry did not arouse the slightest interest. There were glasses with half-finished tea on the table, and a plateful of crumbs. One man in a corner was reading a newspaper. A woman in a grey shawl was sitting at the table with her cheek propped on her hand and a tear-drop on her wrist. Two or three other persons were sitting quite still on the divan. A little girl rather like the one I had seen sleeping was stroking an old dog curled up on a chair. Somebody began to laugh or gasp or something in the adjacent room, where there were more people sitting or wandering about. The boy who had met me in the hall passed carrying a glass of water and I asked him in Russian whether I might speak to Mrs. Helene Grinstein.

"Aunt Elena," he said to the back of a dark slim woman who was bending over an old man hunched up in an armchair. She came up to me and invited me to walk into a small parlour on the other side of the passage. She was very young and graceful with a small powdered face and long soft eyes which appeared to be pulled up towards the temples. She wore a black jumper and her hands were as delicate as her neck.

"Kahk eto oojahsno . . . isn't it dreadful?" She whispered.

I replied rather foolishly that I was afraid I had called at the wrong moment.

"Oh," she said, "I thought" . . . She looked at me. "Sit down," she said, "I thought I saw your face just now at the funeral . . . No? Well, you see, my brother-in-law has died and . . . No, no, sit down. It has been an awful day."

"I don't want to disturb you," I said, "I'd better go . . . I only wanted to talk to you about a relation of mine . . . whom I think you knew . . . at Blauberg . . . but it does not matter . . ."

"Blauberg? I have been there twice," she said and her face twitched as the telephone began ringing somewhere.

"His name was Sebastian Knight," I said looking at her unpainted tender trembling lips.

"No, I have never heard that name," she said, "no."

"He was half-English," I said, "he wrote books."

She shook her head and then turned to the door which had been opened by the sullen boy, her nephew.

"Sonya is coming up in half-an hour," he said. She nodded and he withdrew.

"In fact I did not know any one at the hotel," she continued. I bowed and apologised again.

"But what is *your* name," she asked peering at me with her dim soft eyes which somehow reminded me of Clare. "I think you mentioned it, but to-day my brain seems to be in a daze . . . Ach," she said when I had told her. "But that sounds familiar. Wasn't there a man of that name killed in a duel in St. Petersburg? Oh, your father? I see. Wait a minute. Somebody . . . just the other day . . . somebody had been recalling the case. How funny . . . It always happens like that, in heaps. Yes . . . the Rosanovs . . . They knew your family and all that . . ."

"My brother had a school-fellow called Rosanov," I said.

"You'll find them in the telephone book," she went on rapidly, "you see, I don't know them very well, and I am quite incapable just now of looking up anything."

She was called away and I wandered alone toward the hall. There I found an elderly gentleman pensively sitting on my overcoat and smoking a cigar. At first he could not quite make out what I wanted but then was effusively apologetic.

Somehow I felt sorry it had not been Helene Grinstein. Although of course she never *could* have been the woman who had made Sebastian so miserable. Girls of her type do not smash a man's life—they build it. There she had been steadily managing a house that was bursting with grief and had found it possible to attend to the fantastic affairs of a completely superfluous stranger. And not only had she listened to me, she had given me a tip which I then and there followed, and though the people I saw had nothing to do with Blauberg and the unknown woman, I collected one of the most precious pages of Sebastian's life. A more systematic mind than mine would have placed them in the beginning of this book, but my quest had developed its own magic and logic and though I sometimes cannot help believing that it had gradually grown into a dream, that quest, using the pattern of reality for the weaving of its own fancies, I am forced to recognise that I was being led right, and that in striving to render Sebastian's life I must now follow the same rhythmical interlacements.

There seems to have been a law of some strange harmony in the placing of a meeting relating to Sebastian's first adolescent romance in such close proximity to the echoes of his last dark love. Two modes of his life question each other and the answer is his life itself, and that is the nearest one ever can approach a human truth. He was sixteen and so was she. The lights go out, the curtain rises and a Russian summer landscape is disclosed: the bend of a river half in the shade because of the dark fir trees growing on one steep clay bank and almost reaching out with their deep black reflections to the other side which is low and sunny and sweet, with marsh-flowers and silver-tufted grass. Sebastian, his close-cropped head hatless, his loose silk blouse now clinging to his shoulder-blades, now to his chest according to whether he bends or leans back, is lustily rowing in a boat painted a shiny green. A girl is sitting at the helm, but we shall let her remain achromatic: a mere outline, a white shape not filled in with colour by the artist. Dark blue dragonflies in a slow skipping flight pass hither and thither and alight on the flat waterlily leaves. Names, dates and even faces have been hewn in the red clay of the steeper bank and swifts dart in and out of holes therein. Sebastian's teeth glisten. Then, as he pauses and looks back, the boat with a silky swish slides into the rushes.

"You're a very poor cox," he says.

The picture changes: another bend of that river. A path leads to the water edge, stops, hesitates and turns to loop around a rude bench. It is not quite evening yet, but the air is golden and midgets are performing a primitive native dance in a sunbeam between the aspen leaves which are quite quite still at last, forgetful of Judas.

Sebastian is sitting upon the bench and reading aloud some English verse from a black copybook. Then he stops suddenly: a little to the left a naiad's head with auburn hair is seen just above the water, receding slowly, the long tresses floating behind. Then the nude bather emerges on the opposite bank, blowing his nose with the aid of his thumb; it is the long-haired village priest. Sebastian goes on reading to the girl beside him. The painter has not yet filled in the white space except for a thin sunburnt arm streaked from wrist to elbow along its outer side with glistening down.

As in Byron's dream, again the picture changes. It is night. The sky is alive with stars. Years later Sebastian wrote that gazing at the stars gave him a sick and squeamish feeling, as for instance when you look at the bowels of a ripped-up beast. But at the time, this thought of Sebastian's had not yet been expressed. It is very dark. Nothing can be discerned of what is possibly an alley in the park. Sombre mass on sombre mass and somewhere an owl hooting. An abyss of blackness where all of a sudden a small greenish circle moves up: the luminous dial of a watch (Sebastian disapproved of watches in his riper years).

"Must you go?" asks his voice.

A last change: a V-shaped flight of migrating cranes; their tender moan melting in a turquoise-blue sky high above a tawny birch-grove. Sebastian, still not alone, is seated on the white-and-cinder-grey trunk of a felled tree. His bicycle rests, its spokes a-glitter among the bracken. A Camberwell Beauty skims past and settles on the kerf, fanning its velvety wings. Back to town to-morrow, school beginning on Monday.

"Is this the end? Why do you say that we shall not see each other this winter?" he asks for the second or third time. No answer. "Is it true that you think you've fallen in love with that student chap?—*vetovo studenta?*" The seated girl's shape remains blank except for the arm and a thin brown hand toying with a bicycle pump. With the end of the holder it slowly writes on the soft earth the word "yes," in English, to make it gentler.

The curtain is rung down. Yes, that is all. It is very little but it is heartbreaking. Never more may he ask of the boy who sits daily at the next school desk, "And how is your sister?" Nor must he ever question old Miss Forbes, who still drops in now and then, about the little girl to whom she had also given lessons. And how shall he tread again the same paths next summer, and watch the sunset and cycle down to the river? (But next summer was mainly devoted to the futurist poet Pan.)

By a chance conjuncture of circumstances it was Natasha Rosanov's brother that drove me to the Charlottenburg station to catch the Paris express. I said how curious it had been to have talked to his sister, now the plump mother of two boys, about a distant summer in the dreamland of Russia. He answered that he was perfectly content with his job in Berlin. I tried, as I had vainly tried before, to make him talk of Sebastian's school life. "My memory is appallingly bad," he replied, "and anyway I am too busy to be sentimental about such ordinary things."

"Oh, but surely, surely," I said, "you can recall some little outstanding fact, anything would be welcome . . ." He laughed. "Well," he said, "haven't you just spent hours talking to my sister? She adores the past, doesn't she? She says, you are going to put her in a book as she was in those days, she is quite looking forward to it, in fact."

"Please, try and remember something," I insisted stubbornly.

"I am telling you that I do not remember, you queer person. It's useless, quite useless. There is nothing to relate except ordinary rot about cribbing and cramming and nicknaming teachers. We had quite a good time, I suppose . . . But you know, your brother . . . how shall I put it? . . . your brother was not very popular at school . . ."

THE REAL LIFE OF SEBASTIAN KNIGHT

AS THE reader may have noticed, I have tried to put into this book as little of my own self as possible. I have tried not to allude (though a hint now and then might have made the background of my research somewhat clearer) to the circumstances of my own life. So at this point of my story I shall not dwell upon certain business difficulties I experienced on my arrival in Paris, where I had a more or less permanent home; they were in no way related to my quest, and if I mention them in passing, it is only to stress the fact that I was so engrossed in the attempt to discover Sebastian's last love that I cheerfully dismissed any personal troubles which my taking such a long holiday might entail.

I was not sorry that I had started off with the Berlin clue. It had at least led me to obtain an unexpected glimpse of another chapter of Sebastian's past. And now one name was erased, and I had three more chances before me. The Paris telephone directory yielded the information that "Graun (von), Helene" and "Rechnoy, Paul" (the "de," I noticed, was absent) corresponded to the addresses I possessed. The prospect of meeting a husband was unpleasant but unavoidable. The third lady, Lydia Bohemsky, was ignored by both directories, that is the telephone book and that other Bottin masterpiece, where addresses are arranged according to streets. Anyway, the address I had might help me to get at her. I knew my Paris well, so that I saw at once the most time-saving sequence in which to dispose my calls if I wanted to have done with them in one day. Let it be added, in case the reader be surprised at the rough-and-ready style of my activity, that I dislike telephoning as much as I do writing letters.

The door at which I rang was opened by a lean, tall, shock-headed man in his shirtsleeves and with a brass stud at his collarless throat. He held a chessman—a black knight—in his hand. I greeted him in Russian.

"Come in, come in," he said cheerfully, as if he had been expecting me.

"My name is so-and-so," I said.

"And mine," he cried, "is Pahl Pahlich Rechnoy,"—and he guffawed heartily as if it were a good joke. "If you please," he said, pointing with the chessman to an open door.

I was ushered into a modest room, with a sewing machine standing in one corner and a faint smell of ribbon-and-linen in the air. A heavily built man was sitting sideways at a table on which an oilcloth chessboard was spread, with pieces too large for the squares. He looked at them askance while the empty cigarette-holder in the corner of his mouth looked the other way. A pretty little boy of four or five was kneeling on the floor, surrounded by tiny motor cars. Pahl Pahlich chucked the black knight onto the table and its head came off. Black carefully screwed it on again.

"Sit down," said Pahl Pahlich. "This is my cousin," he added. Black bowed. I sat down on the third (and last) chair. The child came up to me and silently showed me a new red-and-blue pencil.

"I could take your rook now if I wished," said Black darkly, "but I have a much better move."

142

He lifted his queen and delicately crammed it into a cluster of yellowish pawns—one of which was represented by a thimble.

Pahl Pahlich made a lightning swoop and took the queen with his bishop. Then he roared with laughter.

"And now," said Black calmly, when White had stopped roaring, "now you are in the soup. Check, my dove."

While they were arguing over the position, with White trying to take his move back, I looked round the room. I noted the portrait of what had been in the past an Imperial Family. And the moustache of a famous general, moscowed a few years ago. I noted, too, the bulging springs of the bug-brown couch, which served, I felt, as a triple bed—for husband and wife and child. For a minute, the object of my coming seemed to me madly absurd. Somehow, too, I remembered Chichikov's round of weird visits in Gogol's "Dead Souls." The little boy was drawing a motor car for me.

"I am at your service," said Pahl Pahlich (he had lost, I saw, and Black was putting the pieces back into an old cardboard box—all except the thimble). I said what I had carefully prepared beforehand: namely that I wanted to see his wife, because she had been friends with some . . . well, German friends of mine. (I was afraid of mentioning Sebastian's name too soon).

"You'll have to wait a bit then," said Pahl Pahlich. "She is busy in town, you see. I think, she'll be back in a moment."

I made up my mind to wait, although I felt that to-day I should hardly manage to see his wife alone. I hoped however that a little deft questioning might at once settle whether she had known Sebastian; then, bye-and-bye, I could make her talk.

"In the meantime," said Pahl Pahlich, "we shall clap down a little brandy—*cognachkoo*."

The child, finding that I had been sufficiently interested in his pictures, wandered off to his uncle, who at once took him on his knee and proceeded to draw with incredible rapidity and very beautifully a racing car.

"You are an artist," I said—to say something.

Pahl Pahlich, who was rinsing glasses in the tiny kitchen, laughed and shouted over his shoulder: "Oh, he's an all round genius. He can play the violin standing upon his head, and he can multiply one telephone number by another in three seconds, and he can write his name upside down in his ordinary hand."

"And he can drive a taxi," said the child, dangling its thin, dirty little legs.

"No, I shan't drink with you," said Uncle Black, as Pahl Pahlich put the glasses on the table. "I think, I shall take the boy out for a walk. Where are his things?"

The boy's coat was found, and Black led him away. Pahl Pahlich poured out the brandy and said: "You must excuse me for these glasses. I was rich in Russia and I got rich again in Belgium ten years ago, but then I went broke. Here's to yours."

"Does your wife sew?" I asked, so as to set the ball rolling.

"Oh, yes, she has taken up dressmaking," he said with a happy laugh. "And I'm a type-setter, but I have just lost my job. She's sure to be back in a moment. I did not know she had German friends," he added.

"I think," I said, "they met her in Germany, or was it Alsace?" He had been refilling his glass eagerly, but suddenly he stopped and looked at me agape.

"I'm afraid, there's some mistake," he exclaimed. "It must have been my first wife. Varvara Mitrofanna has never been out of Paris—except Russia, of course,—she came here from Sebastopol via Marseilles." He drained his glass and began to laugh.

"That's a good one," he said eyeing me curiously. "Have I met you before? Do you know my first one personally?"

I shook my head.

"Then you're lucky," he cried. "Damned lucky. And your German friends have sent you upon a wild goose-chase because you'll never find her."

"Why?" I asked getting more and more interested.

"Because soon after we separated, and that was years ago, I lost sight of her absolutely. Somebody saw her in Rome, and somebody saw her in Sweden,—but I'm not sure even of that. She may be here, and she may be in hell. I don't care."

"And you could not suggest any way of finding her?"

"None," he said

"Mutual acquaintances?"

"They were *her* acquaintances, not mine," he answered with a shudder.

"You haven't got a photo of her or something?"

"Look here," he said, "what are you driving at? Are the police after her? Because, you know, I shouldn't be surprised if she turned out to be an international spy. Mata Hari! That's her type. Oh, absolutely. And then. . . Well, she's not a girl you can easily forget once she's got into your system. She sucked me dry, and in more ways than one. Money and soul, for instance. I would have killed her . . . if it had not been for Anatole."

"And who's that?" I asked.

"Anatole? Oh, that's the executioner. The man with the guillotine here. So you're not of the police, after all. No? Well, it's your own business, I suppose. But, really, she drove me mad. I met her, you know, in Ostende, that must have been, let me see, in 1927,—she was twenty then, no, not even twenty. I knew she was another fellow's mistress and all that, but I did not care. Her idea of life was drinking cocktails, and eating a large supper at four o'clock in the morning, and dancing the shimmy or whatever it was called, and inspecting brothels because that was fashionable among Parisian snobs, and buying expensive clothes, and raising hell in hotels when she thought the maid had stolen her small change which she afterwards found in the bathroom . . . Oh, and all the rest of it,—you may find her in any cheap novel, she's a type, a type. And she loved inventing some rare illness and going to some famous kurort, and . . ."

"Wait a bit," I said, "That interests me. In June, 1929, she was alone in Blauberg."

"Exactly, but that was at the very end of our marriage. We were living in Paris then, and soon after we separated, and I worked for a year at a factory in Lyon. I was broke, you see."

"Do you mean to say she met some man in Blauberg?"

"No, that I don't know. You see, I don't think she really went very far in deceiving me, not really, you know, not the whole hog,—at least I tried to think so, because there were always lots of men around her, and she didn't mind being kissed by them, I suppose, but I should have gone mad, had I let myself brood over the matter. Once, I remember . . ."

"Pardon me," I interrupted again, "but are you quite sure you never heard of an English friend of hers?"

"English? I thought you said German. No, I don't know. There was a young American at Ste. Maxime in 1928, I believe, who almost swooned every time Ninka danced with him,—and, well, there may have been Englishmen at Ostende and elsewhere, but really I never bothered about the nationality of her admirers."

"So you are quite, quite sure that you don't know about Blauberg and . . . well, about what happened afterwards?"

"No," he said. "I don't think that she was interested in anybody there. You see, she had one of her illness-phases at the time—and she used to eat only lemon-ice and cucumbers, and talk of death and the Nirvana or something—she had a weakness for Lhassa—you know what I mean. . ."

"What exactly was her name?" I asked.

"Well, when I met her her name was Nina Toorovetz—but whether——No, I think, you won't find her. As a matter of fact, I often catch myself thinking that she has never existed. I told Varvara Mitrofanna about her, and she said it was merely a bad dream after seeing a bad cinema film. Oh, you are not going yet, are you? She'll be back in a minute . . ." He looked at me and laughed (I think he had had a little too much of that brandy).

"Oh, I forget," he said. "It is not my present wife that you want to find. And by the way," he added, "my papers are in perfect order. I can show you my *carte de travail*. And if you do find her, I should like to see her before she goes to prison. Or perhaps better not."

"Well, thank you for our conversation," I said, as we were, rather too enthusiastically, shaking hands—first in the room, then in the passage, then in the doorway.

"I thank you," Pahl Pahlich cried. "You see, I quite like talking about her and I am sorry I did not keep any of her photographs."

I stood for a moment reflecting. Had I pumped him enough . . . Well, I could always see him once more . . . Might there not be a chance photo in one of those illustrated papers with cars, furs, dogs, Riviera fashions? I asked about that.

"Perhaps," he answered, "perhaps. She got a prize once at a fancy-dress ball, but I don't quite remember where it happened. All towns seemed restaurants and dancing-halls to me."

He shook his head laughing boisterously, and slammed the door. Uncle Black and the child were slowly coming up the stairs as I went down.

"Once upon a time," Uncle Black was saying, "there was a racing motorist who had a little squirrel; and one day . . ."

MY FIRST impression was that I had got what I wanted,—that at least I knew *who* Sebastian's mistress had been; but presently I cooled down. Could it have been she, that wind-bag's first wife? I wondered as a taxi took me to my next address. Was it really worth while following that plausible, too plausible trail? Was not the image Pahl Pahlich had conjured up a trifle too obvious? The whimsical wanton that ruins a foolish man's life. But was Sebastian foolish? I called to mind his acute distaste for the obvious bad and the obvious good; for ready-made forms of pleasure and hackneyed forms of distress. A girl of that type would have got on his nerves immediately. For what could her conversation have been, if indeed she *had* managed to get acquainted with that quiet, unsociable, absent-minded Englishman at the Beaumont hotel? Surely, after the very first airing of her notions, he would have avoided her. He used to say, I know, that fast girls had slow minds and that there could be nothing duller than a pretty woman who likes fun; even more: that if you looked well at the prettiest girl while she was exuding the cream of the commonplace, you were sure to find some minute blemish in her beauty, corresponding to her habits of thought. He would not mind perhaps having a bite at the apple of sin because, apart from solecisms, he was indifferent to the idea of sin; but he did mind apple-jelly, potted and patented. He might have forgiven a woman for being a flirt, but he would never have stood a sham mystery. He might have been amused by a hussy getting drunk on beer, but he could not have tolerated a *grande cocotte* hinting at a craving for bhang. The more I thought of it, the less possible it seemed . . . At any rate, I ought not to bother about that girl until I had examined the two other possibilities.

So it was with an eager step that I entered the very imposing house (in a very fashionable part of the town) at which my taxi had stopped. The maid said Madame was not in but, on seeing my disappointment, asked me to wait a moment and then returned with the suggestion that if I liked, I could talk to Madame von Graun's friend, Madame Lecerf. She turned out to be a small, slight, pale faced young woman with smooth black hair. I thought I had never seen a skin so evenly pale; her black dress was high at the neck, and she used a long black cigarette holder.

"So you would like to see my friend?" she said, and there was, I thought, a delightful old-world suavity in her crystal clear French.

I introduced myself.

"Yes," she said, "I saw your card. You are Russian, aren't you?"

"I have come," I explained, "on a very delicate errand. But first tell me, am I right in assuming that Madame Graun is a compatriot of mine?"

"*Mais oui, elle est tout ce qu'il y a de plus russe,*" she answered in her soft tinkling voice. "Her husband was German, but he spoke Russian, too."

"Ah," I said, "that past tense is most welcome."

"You may be quite frank with me," said Madame Lecerf. "I rather like delicate errands."

"I am related," I went on, "to the English author, Sebastian Knight, who died two months ago; and I am attempting to work out his biography. He had a close friend whom he met at Blauberg where he stayed in 1929. I am trying to trace her. This is about all."

"*Quelle drôle d'histoire!*" she exclaimed. "What a curious story. And what do you want her to tell you?"

"Oh, anything she pleases . . . But am I to understand . . . Do you mean that Madame Graun is the person in question?"

"Very possibly," she said, "though I don't think I ever heard her mentioning that particular name . . . What did you say it was?"

"Sebastian Knight."

"No. But still it's quite possible. She always picks up friends at the places where she stays. *Il va sans dire*," she added, "that you ought to speak to her personally. Oh, I'm sure you'll find her charming. But what a strange story," she repeated looking at me with a smile. "Why must you write a book about him, and how is it you don't know the woman's name?"

"Sebastian Knight was rather secretive," I explained. "And that lady's letters which he kept . . . Well, you see—he wished them destroyed after his death."

"That's right," she said cheerfully, "I quite understand him. By all means, burn love-letters. The past makes noble fuel. Would you like a cup of tea?"

"No," I said. "What I would like is to know when I can see Madame Graun."

"Soon," said Madame Lecerf. "She is not in Paris for the

moment, but I think you might call again to-morrow. Yes, that'll be all right, I suppose. She may even return to-night."

"Might I ask you," I said, "to tell me more about her?"

"Well, that's easy," said Madame Lecerf. "She is quite a good singer, tzigan songs, you know, that kind. She is extraordinarily beautiful. *Elle fait des passions.* I like her awfully and I have a room at this flat whenever I stay in Paris. Here is her picture, by the way."

Slowly and noiselessly she moved across the thick-carpeted drawing room, and took a large framed photograph which was standing on the piano. I stared for a moment at an exquisite face half turned away from me. The soft curve of the cheek and the upward dart of the ghostly eyebrow were very Russian, I thought. There was a gleam on the lower eyelid, and a gleam on the full dark lips. The expression seemed to me a strange mixture of dreaminess and cunning.

"Yes," I said, "yes . . ."

"Why, is it she?" asked Madame Lecerf inquisitively.

"It might be," I replied, "and I am much looking forward to meeting her."

"I'll try to find out myself," said Madame Lecerf with a charming air of conspiracy. "Because, you see, I think writing a book about people you know is so much more honest than making a hash of them and then presenting it as your own invention!"

I thanked her and made my adieux as the French have it. Her hand was remarkably small, and as I inadvertently pressed it too hard, she winced, for there was a big sharp ring on the middle finger. It hurt me too a little.

"To-morrow at the same time," she said and laughed gently. A nice quiet, quietly moving person.

I had learnt really nothing as yet, but I felt I was proceeding successfully. Now it remained to set my mind at ease in regard to Lydia Bohemsky. When I called at the address I had, I was told by the concierge that the lady had moved some months ago. He said he thought she lived at a small hotel across the street. There I was told that she had gone three weeks ago and was living at the other end of the town. I asked my informant whether he thought she was Russian. He said she was. "A handsome dark woman?" I suggested, using an old Sherlock Holmes stratagem. "Exactly," he replied rather putting me off (the right answer would have been: Oh, no, she is an ugly blond). Half an hour later, I entered a gloomy-looking house not far from the Santé prison. My ring was answered by a fat elderly woman with waved bright orange hair, purplish jowls and some dark fluff over her painted lip.

"May I speak to Mademoiselle Lydia Bohemsky?" I said.

"C'est moi," she replied with a terrific Russian accent.

"Then I'll bring the things," I muttered and hurriedly left the house. I sometimes think that she may be still standing in the doorway.

When next day I called again at Madame von Graun's flat, the maid showed me into another room—a kind of boudoir doing its best to look charming. I had already noticed on the day before the intense warmth in the flat—and as the weather outside was, though decidedly damp, yet hardly what you would call chilly, this orgy of central heating seemed rather exaggerated. I was kept waiting a long time. There were several oldish French novels on the console; most of them by literary prize-winners, and a well thumbed copy of Dr. Axel Munthe's *San Michele*. A bunch of carnations stood in a self-conscious vase. There were a few other fragile knick-knacks about—probably quite nice and expensive, but I always have shared Sebastian's almost pathological dislike for anything made of glass or china. Last but not least, there was a sham piece of polished furniture, containing, I felt, that horror of horrors: a radio set. Still, all things considered, Helene von Graun seemed to be a person of "taste and culture."

At last, the door opened and the lady I had seen on the previous day sidled in,—I say sidled because she was turning her head back and down, talking to what turned out to be a frog-faced, wheezing, black bulldog, which seemed reluctant to waddle in.

"Remember my sapphire," she said giving me her little cold hand. She sat down on the blue sofa and pulled up the heavy bull-dog. *"Viens, mon vieux,"* she panted, *"viens.* He is pining away without Helene," she said when the beast was made comfortable among the cushions. "It's a shame, you know, I thought she would be back this morning, but she rang up from Dijon and said she would not arrive till Saturday (today was Tuesday). I'm dreadfully sorry. I did not know where to reach you. Are you very disappointed?"—and she looked at me with her chin on her clasped hands and her sharp elbows in close-fitting velvet propped on her knees.

"Well," I said, "if you tell me something more about Madame Graun, perhaps I may be consoled."

I don't know why, but the atmosphere of the place drove me somehow to affected speech and manner.

"And what is more," she said, lifting a sharp-nailed finger, *"j'ai une petite surprise pour vous.* But first we'll have tea." I saw that I could not avoid the farce of tea this time; indeed, the maid had already wheeled in a movable table with glittering tea things.

"Put it here, Jeanne," said Madame Lecerf. "Yes, that will do."

"Now you must tell me as explicitly as possible," said Madame Lecerf, "*tout ce que vous croyez raisonnable de demander à une tasse de thé.* I suspect you would like some cream in it, if you have lived in England. You *look* English, you know."

"I prefer looking Russian," I said.

"I'm afraid I don't know any Russians, except Helene, of course. These biscuits, I think, are rather amusing."

"And what is your surprise?" I asked.

She had a funny manner of looking at you intently—not into your eyes though, but at the lower part of your face, as if you had got a crumb or something that ought to be wiped off. She was very lightly made up for a French woman, and I thought her transparent skin and dark hair quite attractive.

"Ah!" she said. "I asked her something when she telephoned, and—" she stopped and seemed to enjoy my impatience.

"And she replied," I said, "that she had never heard the name."

"No," said Madame Lecerf, "she just laughed, but I know that laugh of hers."

I got up, I think, and walked up and down the room.

"Well," I said at length, "it is not exactly a laughing matter, is it? Doesn't she know that Sebastian Knight is dead?"

Madame Lecerf closed her dark velvety eyes in a silent "yes" and then looked again at my chin.

"Have you seen her lately,—I mean did you see her in

January when the news of his death was in the papers? Wasn't she sorry?"

"Look here, my dear friend, you are strangely naïve," said Madame Lecerf. "There are many kinds of love and many kinds of sorrow. Let us assume that Helene is the person you are seeking. But why ought we to assume that she loved him enough to be upset by his dying? Or perhaps she did love him, but held special views about death which excluded hysterics? What do we know of such matters? It's her personal affair. She'll tell you, I suppose, but until then it's hardly fair to insult her."

"I did not insult her," I cried. "I am sorry if I sounded unfair. But do talk about her. How long have you known her?"

"Oh, I haven't seen much of her these last years until this one—she travels a lot, you know—but we used to go to the same school—here in Paris. Her father was a Russian painter, I believe. She was still very young when she married that fool."

"What fool?" I queried.

"Well, her husband, of course. Most husbands are fools, but that one was *hors concours*. It didn't last long, happily. Have one of mine." She handed me her lighter too. The bulldog growled in its sleep. She moved and curled up on the sofa, making room for me. "You don't seem to know much about women, do you?" she asked, stroking her own heel.

"I'm only interested in one," I answered.

"And how old are you?" she went on. "Twenty-eight? Have I guessed? No? Oh, well, then you're older than me. But no matter. What was I telling you? . . . I know a few things about her,—what she told me herself and what I have picked up. The only man she really loved was a married man and that was before her marriage, and she was a mere slip of a girl then, mind you—and he got tired of her or something. She had a few affairs after that, but it didn't much matter really. *Un coeur de femme ne ressuscite jamais.* Then there was one story which she told me in full—it was rather a sad one."

She laughed. Her teeth were a little too large for her small pale mouth.

"You look as if my friend were your own sweetheart," she said teasingly. "By the way, I wanted to ask you how did you come to this address—I mean, what led you to look up Helene?"

I told her about the four addresses I had obtained in Blauberg. I mentioned the names.

"That's superb," she cried, "that's what I call energy! *Voyez vous ca!* And you went to Berlin? She was a Jewess? Adorable! And you have found the others too?"

"I saw one," I said, "and that was enough."

"Which?" she asked with a spasm of uncontrollable mirth. "Which? The Rechnoy woman?"

"No," I said. "Her husband has married again, and she has vanished."

"You are charming, charming," said Madame Lecerf, wiping her eyes and rippling with new laughter. "I can see you crashing in and being confronted by an innocent couple. Oh, I never heard anything so funny. Did his wife throw you downstairs, or what?"

"Let us drop the matter," I said rather curtly. I had had enough of that girl's merriment. She had, I am afraid, that French sense of humour in connection with connubial matters, which at another moment might have appealed to me too; but just now I felt that the flippantly indecent view she took of my inquiry was somehow slighting Sebastian's memory. As this feeling deepened, I found myself thinking all of a sudden that perhaps the whole thing was indecent and that my clumsy efforts to hunt down a ghost had swamped any idea that I might ever form of Sebastian's last love. Or would Sebastian have been tickled at the grotesque side of the quest I had undertaken for his sake? Would the biographee have found that special "Knightian twist" about it which would have fully compensated the blundering biographer?

"Please, forgive me," she said, putting her ice-cold hand on mine and looking at me from under her brows. "You must not be so touchy, you know."

She got up quickly and went to the mahogany affair in the corner. I looked at her thin girlish back as she bent down,—and I guessed what she was about to do.

"No, not that, for God's sake!" I cried.

"No?" she said. "I thought a little music might soothe you. And generally create the right atmosphere for our talk. No? Well, just as you like."

The bull-dog shook himself and lay down again.

"That's right," she said in a coaxing-and-pouting voice.

"You were about to tell me," I reminded her.

"Yes," she said sitting down again at my side and pulling at the hem of her skirt, as she curled one leg under her. "Yes. You see, I don't know who the man was, but I gathered he was a difficult sort of man. She says she liked his looks and his hands and his manner of talking, and she thought it would be rather good fun to have him make love to her—because, you see, he looked so very intellectual, and it is always entertaining to see that kind of refined, distant,—brainy fellow suddenly go on all fours and wag his tail. What's the matter now, *cher Monsieur?*"

"What on earth are you talking about?" I cried. "When ... When and where did it happen, that affair?"

"*Ah non merci, je ne suis pas le calendrier de mon amie. Vous ne voudriez pas!* I didn't bother about asking her dates and names, and if she told me them herself, I have forgotten. Now, please, don't ask me any more questions: I am telling you what *I* know, and not what *you'd* like to know. I don't think he was a relation of yours, because he was so unlike you—of course, as far as I can judge by what she told me and by what I have seen of you. You are a nice eager boy—and he, well, he was anything but nice—he got positively wicked when he found out that he was falling in love with Helene. Oh no, *he* did not turn into a sentimental pup, as she had expected. He told her bitterly that she was cheap and vain, and then he kissed her to make sure that she was not a porcelain figure. Well, she wasn't. And presently he found out that he could not live without her, and presently she found out that she had had quite enough of hearing him talk of his dreams, and the dreams in his dreams, and the dreams in the dreams of his dreams. Mind you, I do not condemn either. Perhaps both were right and perhaps neither,—but, you see, my friend was not quite the ordinary woman he thought she was—oh, she was something quite different, and she knew a bit more about life and death and people than he thought he knew. He was the kind of man, you know, who thinks all modern books are trashy, and all modern young people fools, merely because he is much too preoccupied with his own sensations and ideas to understand those of others. She says, you can't imagine his tastes and his whims, and the way he spoke of religion,—it must have been appalling, I suppose. And my friend, you know, is, or rather was, very gay, *très vive*, and all that, but she felt she was getting old and sour whenever he arrived. Because he never stayed long with her, you know,— he would come *à l'improviste* and plump down on a pouf with his hands on the knob of his cane, without taking off his gloves—and stare gloomily. She got friendly with another man soon, who worshipped her and was oh, much, much more attentive and kind and thoughtful than the man you wrongly suppose to have been your brother (don't scowl, please), but she did not much care for either and she says it was a scream to see the way they were polite to each other when they met. She liked travelling, but whenever she found some really nice place, where she could forget her troubles and everything, there he would blot out the landscape again, and sit down on the terrace at her table, and say that she was vain and cheap, and that he could not live without her. Or else, he would make a long speech in front of her friends— you know, *des jeunes gens qui aiment à rigoler*—some long and obscure speech about the form of an ashtray or the colour of time,—and there he would be left on that chair all alone, smiling foolishly to himself, or counting his own pulse. I'm sorry if he really turns out to be your relative because I don't think that she has retained a particularly pleasant souvenir of those days. He became quite a pest at last, she says, and she didn't even let him touch her anymore, because he would have a fit or something when he got excited. One day, at last, when she knew he was going to arrive by the night train, she asked a young man who would do anything to please her, to meet him and tell him that she did not want to see him ever again, and that if he attempted to see her, he would be regarded by her friends as a troublesome stranger and dealt with accordingly. It was not very nice of her, I think, but she supposed it would be better for him in the long run. And it worked. He did not even send her any more of his usual entreating letters, which she never read, anyway. No, no, really, I don't think it can be the man in question,— if I tell you all this it is merely because I want to give you a portrait of Helene—and not of her lovers. She was so full of life, so ready to be sweet to everybody, so brimming with that *vitalité joyeuse qui est, d'ailleurs, tout-à-fait conforme à une philosophie innée, à un sens quasi-religieux des phénomènes de la vie.* And what did it amount to? The men she liked proved dismal disappointments, all women with a very few exceptions were nothing but cats, and she spent the best part of her life in trying to be happy in a world which did its best to break her. Well, you'll meet her and see for yourself whether the world has succeeded.".

We were silent for quite a long time. Alas, I had no more doubts, though the picture of Sebastian was atrocious,—but then, too, I had got it secondhand.

"Yes," I said, "I shall see her at all costs. And this for two reasons. Firstly, because I want to ask her a certain question, —one question only. And secondly . . ."

"Yes?" said Madame Lecerf sipping her cold tea. "Secondly?"

"Secondly, I am at a loss to imagine how such a woman could attract my brother; so I want to see her with my own eyes."

"Do you mean to say," asked Madame Lecerf, "that you

think she is a dreadful, dangerous woman? *Une femme fatale?* Because, you know, that's not so. She's good as good bread."

"Oh, no," I said. "Not dreadful, not dangerous. Clever, if you like, and all that. But . . . No, I must see for myself."

"He who will live will see," said Madame Lecerf. "Now, look here, I've got a suggestion. I am going away to-morrow. I am afraid that if you drop in here on Saturday, Helene may be in such a rush—she is always rushing, you know,—that she'll put you off till next day, forgetting that next day she is coming for a week to my place in the country: so you'll miss her again. In other words, I think that the best thing would be for you to come down to my place, too. Because then you are quite, quite sure to meet her. So, what I suggest is that you come Sunday morning—and stay as long as you choose. We've got four spare bedrooms, and I think you'll be comfortable. And then, you know, if I talk to her first a little, she'll be just in the right mood for a talk with you. *Eh bien, êtes-vous d'accord?*"

VERY curious, I mused: there seemed to be a slight family likeness between Nina Rechnoy and Helene von Graun,—or at least between the two pictures which the husband of one and the friend of the other had painted for me. Between the two there was not much to choose, Nina was shallow and glamourous, Helene cunning and hard; both were flighty; neither was much to my taste,— nor should I have thought to Sebastian's. I wondered if the two women had known each other at Blauberg: they would have gone rather well together,—theoretically; in reality they would probably have hissed and spat at each other. On the other hand, I could now drop the Rechnoy clue altogether—and that was a great relief. What that French girl had told me about her friend's lover could hardly have been a coincidence. Whatever the feelings I experienced at learning the way Sebastian had been treated, I could not help being satisfied that my enquiry was nearing its end and that I was spared the impossible task of unearthing Pahl Pahlich's first wife, who for all I knew might be in jail or in Los Angeles.

I knew I was being given my last chance, and as I was anxious to make sure I would get at Helene von Graun, I made a tremendous effort and sent her a letter to her Paris address, so that she might find it on her arrival. It was quite short: I merely informed her that I was her friend's guest at Lescaux and had accepted this invitation with the sole object of meeting her; I added that there was an important piece of literary business which I wished to discuss with her. This last sentence was not very honest, but I thought it sounded enticing. I had not quite understood whether her friend had told her anything about my desire to see her when she telephoned from Dijon. I was desperately afraid that on Sunday Madame Lecerf might blandly inform me that Helene had left for Nice instead. After posting that letter I felt that at any rate I had done all in my power to fix our rendezvous.

I started at nine in the morning, so as to reach Lescaux around noon as arranged. I was already boarding the train when I realised with a shock that on my way I would pass St. Damier where Sebastian had died and was buried. Here I had travelled one unforgettable night. But now I failed to recognize anything: when the train stopped for a minute at the little St. Damier platform, its inscription alone told me that I had been there. The place looked so simple and staid and definite compared to the distorted dream impression which lingered in my memory. Or was it distorted now?

I felt strangely relieved when the train moved on: no more was I treading the ghostly tracks I had followed two months before. The weather was fair and every time the train stopped I seemed to hear the light uneven breathing of spring, still barely visible but unquestionably present: "cold-limbed ballet-girls waiting in the wings," as Sebastian put it once.

Madame Lecerf's house was large and ramshackle. A score of unhealthy old trees represented the park. There were fields on one side and a hill with a factory on the other. Everything about the place had a queer look of weariness, and shabbiness, and dustiness; when later I learned that it had only been built some thirty-odd years ago I felt still more surprised by its decrepitude. As I approached the main entrance I met a man hastily scrunching down the gravel walk; he stopped and shook hands with me:

"*Enchanté de vous connaître,*" he said, summing me up with a melancholy glance, "my wife is expecting you. *Je suis navré* . . . but I am obliged to go to Paris this Sunday."

He was a middle-aged rather common-looking Frenchman with tired eyes and an automatic smile. We shook hands once more.

"*Mon ami,* you'll miss that train," came Madame Lecerf's crystal voice from the veranda, and he trotted off obediently.

To-day she wore a beige dress, her lips were brightly made up but she had not dreamt of meddling with her diaphanous complexion. The sun gave a blueish sheen to her hair and I found myself thinking that she was after all quite a pretty young woman. We wandered through two or three rooms which looked as if the idea of a drawing-room had been vaguely divided between them. I had the impression that we were quite alone in that unpleasant rambling house. She picked up a shawl lying on a green silk settee and drew it about her.

"Isn't it cold," she said. "That's one thing I hate in life, cold. Feel my hands. They are always like that except in summer. Lunch will be ready in a minute. Sit down."

"When exactly is she coming?" I asked.

"*Ecoutez,*" said Madame Lecerf, "can't you forget her for a minute and talk to me about other things? *Ce n'est pas très poli, vous savez.* Tell me something about yourself. Where do you live, and what do you do?"

"Will she be here in the afternoon?"

"Yes, yes, you obstinate man, *Monsieur l'entêté.* She's

sure to come. Don't be so impatient. You know, women don't much care for men with an *idée fixe*. How did you like my husband?"

I said that he must be much older than she.

"He is quite kind but a dreadful bore," she went on, laughing. "I sent him away on purpose. We've been married for only a year, but it feels like a diamond wedding already. And I just hate this house. Don't you?"

I said it seemed rather old-fashioned.

"Oh, that's not the right term. It looked brand new when I first saw it. But it has faded and crumbled away since. I once told a doctor that all flowers except pinks and daffodils withered if I touched them,—isn't it bizarre?"

"And what did he say?"

"He said he wasn't a botanist. There used to be a Persian princess like me. She blighted the Palace Gardens."

An elderly and rather sullen maid looked in and nodded to her mistress.

"Come along," said Madame Lecerf. *"Vous devez mourir de faim*, judging by your face."

We collided in the doorway because she suddenly turned back as I was following her. She clutched my shoulder and her hair brushed my cheek. "You clumsy young man," she said, "I have forgotten my pills."

She found them and we went over the house in search of the dining-room. We found it at last. It was a dismal place with a bay-window which had seemed to change its mind at the last moment and had made a half-hearted attempt to revert to an ordinary state. Two people drifted in silently, through different doors. One was an old lady who, I gathered, was a cousin of Monsieur Lecerf. Her conversation was strictly limited to polite purrs when passing eatables. The other was a rather handsome man in plus-fours with a solemn face and a queer grey streak in his fair sparse hair. He never uttered a single word during the whole lunch. Madame Lecerf's manner of introducing consisted of a hurried gesture which did not bother about names. I noticed that she ignored his presence at table,—that indeed he seemed to sit apart. The lunch was well-cooked but haphazard. The wine, however, was quite good.

After we had clattered through the first course the blond gentleman lit a cigarette and wandered away. He came back in a minute with an ashtray. Madame Lecerf who had been engaged with her food now looked at me and said:

"So you have travelled a good deal, lately? I have never been to England you know,—somehow it never happened. It seems to be a dull place. *On doit s'y ennuyer follement, n'est-ce-pas?* And then the fogs . . . And no music, no art of any sort . . . This is a special way of preparing rabbit, I think you will like it."

"By the way," I said, "I forgot to tell you, I've written a letter to your friend warning her I would be down here and . . . sort of reminding her to come."

Madame Lecerf put down knife and fork. She looked surprised and annoyed. "You haven't!" she exclaimed.

"But it can't do any harm, can it, or do you think—"

We finished the rabbit in silence. Chocolate cream followed. The blond gentleman carefully folded his napkin, inserted it into a ring, got up, bowed slightly to our hostess and withdrew.

"We shall take our coffee in the green room," said Madame Lecerf to the maid.

"I am furious with you," she said as we settled down. "I think you have spoiled it all."

"Why, what have I done?" I asked.

She looked away. Her small hard bosom heaved (Sebastian once wrote that it happened only in books but here was proof that he was mistaken). The blue vein on her pale girlish neck seemed to throb (but of that I am not so sure). Her lashes fluttered. Yes, she was decidedly a pretty woman. Did she come from the Midi, I wondered. From Arles perhaps. But no, her accent was Parisian.

"Were you born in Paris?" I asked.

"Thank you," she said without looking, "that's the first question you've asked about me. But that does not atone for your blunder. It was the silliest thing you could have done. Perhaps, if I tried . . . Excuse me, I'll be back in a minute."

I sat back and smoked. Dust was swarming in a slanting sunbeam; volutes of tobacco-smoke joined it and rotated softly, insinuatingly, as if they might form a live picture at any moment. Let me repeat here that I am loth to trouble these pages with any kind of matter relating personally to me; but I think it may amuse the reader (and who knows, Sebastian's ghost too) if I say that for a moment I thought of making love to that woman. It was really very odd,—at the same time she got rather on my nerves,—I mean the things she said. I was losing my grip somehow. I shook myself mentally as she returned.

"Now you've done it," she said. "Helene is not at home."

"*Tant mieux,*" I replied, "she's probably on her way here, and really you ought to understand how terribly impatient I am to see her."

"But why on earth did you have to write to her!" Madame

Lecerf cried. "You don't even know her. And I had promised you she would be here to-day. What more could you wish? And if you didn't believe me, if you wanted to control me— *alors vous êtes ridicule, cher Monsieur.*"

"Oh, look here," I said quite sincerely, "that never entered my head. I only thought, well . . . butter can't spoil the porridge, as we Russians say."

"I think I don't much care for butter . . . or Russians," she said. What could I do? I glanced at her hand lying near mine. It was trembling slightly, her frock was flimsy—and a queer little shiver not exactly of cold passed down my spine. Ought I to kiss that hand? Could I manage to achieve courteousness without feeling rather a fool?

She sighed and stood up.

"Well, there's nothing to be done about it. I'm afraid you have put her off and if she does come—well, no matter. We shall see. Would you like to go over our domain? I think it is warmer outside than in this miserable house—*que dans cette triste demeure.*"

The "domain" consisted of the garden and grove I had already noticed. It was all very still. The black branches, here and there studded with green, seemed to be listening to their own inner life. Something dreary and dull hung over the place. Earth had been dug out and heaped against a brick wall by a mysterious gardener who had gone and forgotten his rusty spade. For some odd reason I recalled a murder that had happened lately, a murderer who had buried his victim in just such a garden as this.

Madame Lecerf was silent; then she said: "You must have been very fond of your half-brother, if you make such a fuss about his past. How did he die? Suicide?"

"Oh, no," I said, "he suffered from heart-disease."

"I thought you said he had shot himself. That would have been so much more romantic. I'll be disappointed in your book if it all ends in bed. There are roses here in summer,— here, on that mud,—but catch me spending the summer here ever again."

"I shall certainly never think of falsifying his life in any way," I said.

"Oh, all right. I knew a man who published the letters of his dead wife and distributed them among his friends. Why do you suppose the biography of your brother will interest people?"

"Haven't you ever read"—I began, when suddenly a smart-looking though rather mud-bespattered car stopped at the gate.

"Oh, bother," said Madame Lecerf.

"Perhaps it's she," I exclaimed.

A woman had scrambled out of the car right into a puddle.

"Yes, it's she all right," said Madame Lecerf. "Now you stay where you are, please."

She ran down the path, waving her hand, and upon reaching the newcomer, kissed her and led her to the left where they both disappeared behind a clump of bushes. I espied them again a moment later when they had skirted the garden and were going up the steps. They vanished into the house. I had really seen nothing of Helene von Graun except her unfastened fur coat and bright-coloured scarf.

I found a stone bench and sat down. I was excited and rather pleased with myself for having captured my prey at last. Somebody's cane was lying on the bench and I poked the rich brown earth. I had succeeded! This very night after talking to her I would return to Paris, and . . . A thought strange to the rest, a changeling, a trembling oaf, slipped in, mingling with the crowd . . . Would I return to-night? How was it, that breathless phrase in that second-rate Maupassant story: "I have forgotten a book." But I was forgetting mine too.

"So that's where you are," said Madame Lecerf's voice. "I thought perhaps you had gone home."

"Well, is everything all right?"

"Far from it," she answered calmly. "I have no idea what you wrote, but she thought it referred to a film affair she's trying to arrange. She says you've entrapped her. Now you'll do what I tell you. You won't speak to her to-day or to-morrow or the day after. But you'll stay here and be very nice to her. And she has promised to tell me everything, and afterwards perhaps you may talk to her. Is that a bargain?"

"It's really awfully good of you to take all this trouble," I said.

She sat down on the bench beside me, and as the bench was very short and I am rather—well—on the sturdy side—her shoulder touched mine. I moistened my lips with my tongue and scrawled lines on the ground with the stick I was holding.

"What are you trying to draw?" she asked and then cleared her throat.

"My thought-waves," I answered foolishly.

"Once upon a time," she said softly, "I kissed a man just because he could write his name upside down."

The stick dropped from my hand. I stared at Madame Lecerf. I stared at her smooth white brow, I saw her violet dark eyelids, which she had lowered, possibly mistaking my stare,

—saw a tiny pale birth-mark on the pale cheek, the delicate wings of her nose, the pucker of her upper lip, as she bent her dark head, the dull whiteness of her throat, the laquered rose-red nails of her thin fingers. She lifted her face, her queer velvety eyes with that iris placed slightly higher than usual, looked at my lips.

I got up.

"What's the matter," she said, "what are you thinking about?"

I shook my head. But she was right. I was thinking of something now—something that had to be solved, at once.

"Why, are we going in?" she asked as we moved up the path.

I nodded.

"But she won't be down before another minute, you know. Tell me why you are sulking?"

I think I stopped and stared at her again, this time at her slim little figure in that buff, close fitting frock.

I moved on, brooding heavily, and the sun-dappled path seemed to frown back at me.

"*Vous n'êtes guère aimable,*" said Madame Lecerf.

There was a table and several chairs on the terrace. The silent blond person whom I had seen at lunch was sitting there examining the works of his watch. As I sat down I clumsily jolted his elbow and he let drop a tiny screw.

"*Boga radi,*" he said (don't mention it) as I apologised.

(Oh, he was Russian, was he? Good, that would help me.)

The lady stood with her back to us, humming gently, her foot tapping the stone flags.

It was then that I turned to my silent compatriot who was ogling his broken watch.

"*Ah-oo-neigh na-sheiky pah-ook,*" I said softly.

The lady's hand flew up to the nape of her neck, she turned on her heel.

"Shto?" (what?) asked my slow-minded compatriot, glancing at me. Then he looked at the lady, grinned uncomfortably and fumbled with his watch.

"*J'ai quelque chose dans le cou . . .* There's something on my neck, I feel it," said Madame Lecerf.

"As a matter of fact," I said, "I have just been telling this Russian gentleman that I thought there was a spider on your neck. But I was mistaken, it was a trick of light."

"Shall we put on the gramophone?" she asked brightly.

"I'm awfully sorry," I said, "but I think I must be going home. You'll excuse me won't you?"

"*Mais vous êtes fou,*" she cried, "you are mad, don't you want to see my friend?"

"Another time perhaps," I said soothingly, "another time."

"Tell me," she said following me into the garden, "what *is* the matter?"

"It was very clever of you," I said, in our liberal grand Russian language, "it was very clever of you to make me believe you were talking about your friend when all the time you were talking about yourself. This little hoax would have gone on for quite a long time if fate had not pushed your elbow, and now you've spilled the curds and whey. Because I happen to have met your former husband's cousin, the one who could write upside down. So I made a little test. And when you subconsciously caught the Russian sentence I muttered aside. . . ." No, I did not say a word of all this. I just bowed myself out of the garden. She will be sent a copy of this book and will understand.

THAT question which I had wished to ask Nina remained unuttered. I had wished to ask her whether she ever realised that the wan-faced man, whose presence she had found so tedious, was one of the most remarkable writers of his time. What was the use of asking! Books mean nothing to a woman of her kind; her own life seems to her to contain the thrills of a hundred novels. Had she been condemned to spend a whole day shut up in a library, she would have been found dead about noon. I am quite sure that Sebastian never alluded to his work in her presence: it would have been like discussing sundials with a bat. So let us leave that bat to quiver and wheel in the deepening dusk: the clumsy mimic of a swallow.

In those last and saddest years of his life Sebastian wrote *The Doubtful Asphodel*, which is unquestionably his masterpiece. Where and how did he write it? In the reading-room of the British Museum (far from Mr. Goodman's vigilant eye). At a humble table deep in the corner of a Parisian "bistro" (not of the kind that his mistress might patronise). In a deck-chair under an orange parasol somewhere in Cannes or Juan, when she and her gang had deserted him for a spree elsewhere. In the waiting-room of an anonymous station, between two heart-attacks. In a hotel, to the clatter of plates being washed in the yard. In many other places which I can but vaguely conjecture. The theme of the book is simple: a man is dying: you feel him sinking throughout the book; his thought and his memories pervade the whole with greater or lesser distinction (like the swell and fall of uneven breathing), now rolling up this image, now that, letting it ride in the wind, or even tossing it out on the shore, where it seems to move and live for a minute on its own and presently is drawn back again by grey seas where it sinks or is strangely transfigured. A man is dying, and he is the hero of the tale; but whereas the lives of other people in the book seem perfectly realistic (or at least realistic in a Knightian sense), the reader is kept ignorant as to who the dying man is, and where his deathbed stands or floats, or whether it is a bed at all. The man is the book; the book itself is heaving and dying, and drawing up a ghostly knee. One thought-image, then another breaks upon the shore of consciousness, and we follow the thing or the being that has been evoked: stray remnants of a wrecked life; sluggish fancies which crawl and then unfurl eyed wings. They are, these lives, but commentaries to the main subject. We follow the gentle old chess player Schwarz, who sits down on a chair in a room in a house, to teach an orphan boy the moves of the knight; we meet the fat Bohemian woman with that grey streak showing in the fast colour of her cheaply dyed hair; we listen to a pale wretch noisily denouncing the policy of oppression to an attentive plainclothes man in an ill-famed public-house. The lovely tall primadonna steps in her haste into a puddle, and her silver shoes are ruined. An old man sobs and is soothed by a soft-lipped girl in mourning. Professor Nussbaum, a Swiss scientist, shoots his young mistress and himself dead in a hotel-room at half past three in the morning. They come and go, these and other people, opening and shutting doors, living as long as the way they follow is lit, and are engulfed in turn by the waves of the dominant theme: a man is dying. He seems to move an arm or turn his head on what might be a pillow, and as he moves, this or that life we have just been watching, fades or changes. At moments, his personality grows conscious of itself, and then we feel that we are passing down some main artery of the book. "Now, when it was too late, and Life's shops were closed, he regretted not having bought a certain book he had always wanted; never having gone through an earthquake, a fire, a train-accident; never having seen Tatsienlu in Tibet, or heard blue magpies chattering in Chinese willows; not having spoken to that errant schoolgirl with shameless eyes, met one day in a lonely glade; not having laughed at the poor little joke of a shy ugly woman, when no one had laughed in the room; having missed trains, allusions and opportunities; not having handed the penny he had in his pocket to that old street-violinist playing to himself tremulously on a certain bleak day in a certain forgotten town."

Sebastian Knight had always liked juggling with themes, making them clash or blending them cunningly, making *them* express that hidden meaning, which could only be expressed in a succession of waves, as the music of a Chinese buoy can be made to sound only by undulation. In *The Doubtful Asphodel*, his method has attained perfection. It is not the parts that matter, it is their combinations.

There seems to be a method, too, in the author's way of expressing the physical process of dying: the steps leading into darkness; action being taken in turns by the brain, the flesh, the lungs. First the brain follows up a certain hierarchy of ideas—ideas about death: sham-clever thoughts scribbled in the margin of a borrowed book (the episode of the philosopher): "Attraction of death: physical growth considered upside down as the lengthening of a suspended drop; at last falling into nothing." Thoughts, poetical, religious: ". . . the swamp of rank materialism and the golden paradises of those whom Dean Park calls the optimystics . . ." "But the dying man knew that these were not real ideas; that only one half of the notion of death can be said really to exist: *this* side of the question—the wrench, the parting, the quay of life gently moving away aflutter with handkerchiefs: ah! he was already on the other side, if he could see the beach receding; no, not quite—if he was still thinking." (Thus, one who has come to see a friend away, may stay on deck too late, but still not become a traveller.)

Then, little by little, the demons of physical sickness smother with mountains of pain all kinds of thought, philosophy, surmise, memories, hope, regret. We stumble and crawl through hideous landscapes, nor do we mind where we go—because it is all anguish and nothing but anguish. The method is now reversed. Instead of those thought-images which radiated fainter and fainter, as we followed them down blind alleys, it is now the slow assault of horrible uncouth visions drawing upon us and hemming us in: the story of a tortured child; an exile's account of life in the cruel country whence he fled; a meek lunatic with a black eye; a farmer kicking his dog—lustily, wickedly. Then the pain fades too. "Now he was left so exhausted that he failed to be interested in death." Thus "sweaty men snore in a crowded third-class carriage; thus a schoolboy falls asleep over his unfinished sum." "I am tired, tired . . . a tyre rolling and rolling by itself, now wobbling, now slowing down, now . . ."

177

This is the moment when a wave of light suddenly floods the book: ". . . as if somebody had flung open the door and people in the room have started up, blinking, feverishly picking up parcels." We feel that we are on the brink of some absolute truth, dazzling in its splendour and at the same time almost homely in its perfect simplicity. By an incredible feat of suggestive wording, the author makes us believe that he knows the truth about death and that he is going to tell it. In a moment or two, at the end of this sentence, in the middle of the next, or perhaps a little further still, we shall learn something that will change all our concepts, as if we discovered that by moving our arms in some simple, but never yet attempted manner, we could fly. "The hardest knot is but a meandering string; tough to the finger nails, but really a matter of lazy and graceful loopings. The eye undoes it, while clumsy fingers bleed. He (the dying man) was that knot, and he would be untied at once, if he could manage to see and follow the thread. And not only himself, everything would be unravelled,—everything that he might imagine in our childish terms of space and time, both being riddles invented by man *as* riddles, and thus coming back at us: the boomerangs of nonsense . . . Now he had caught something real, which had nothing to do with any of the thoughts or feelings, or experiences he might have had in the kindergarten of life . . ."

The answer to all questions of life and death, "the absolute solution" was written all over the world he had known: it was like a traveller realising that the wild country he surveys is not an accidental assembly of natural phenomena, but the page in a book where these mountains and forests, and fields, and rivers are disposed in such a way as to form a coherent sentence; the vowel of a lake fusing with the consonant of a sibilant slope; the windings of a road writing its message in a round hand, as clear as that of one's father; trees conversing in dumb-show, making sense to one who has learnt the gestures of their language . . . Thus the traveller spells the landscape and its sense is disclosed, and likewise, the intricate pattern of human life turns out to be monogrammatic, now quite clear to the inner eye disentangling the interwoven letters. And the word, the meaning which appears is astounding in its simplicity: the greatest surprise being perhaps that in the course of one's earthly existence, with one's brain encompassed by an iron ring, by the close-fitting dream of one's own personality—one had not made by chance that simple mental jerk, which would have set free imprisoned thought and granted it the great understanding. Now the puzzle was solved. "And as the meaning of all things shone through their shapes, many ideas and events which had seemed of the utmost importance dwindled not to insignificance, for nothing could be insignificant now, but to the same size which other ideas and events, once denied any importance, now attained." Thus, such shining giants of our brain as science, art or religion fell out of the familiar scheme of their classification, and joining hands, were mixed and joyfully levelled. Thus, a cherry stone and its tiny shadow which lay on the painted wood of a tired bench, or a bit of torn paper, or any other such trifle out of millions and millions of trifles grew to a wonderful size. Remodelled and re-combined, the world yielded its sense to the soul as naturally as both breathed.

And now we shall know what exactly it is; the word will be uttered—and you, and I, and every one in the world will slap himself on the forehead: What fools we have been! At this last bend of his book the author seems to pause for a minute, as if he were pondering whether it were wise to let the truth out. He seems to lift his head and to leave the dying man, whose thoughts he was following, and to turn away and to think: Shall we follow him to the end? Shall we whisper the word which will shatter the snug silence of our brains? We shall. We have gone too far as it is, and the word is being already formed, and will come out. And we turn and bend again over a hazy bed, over a grey, floating form,—lower and lower . . . But that minute of doubt was fatal: the man is dead.

The man is dead and we do not know. The asphodel on the other shore is as doubtful as ever. We hold a dead book in our hands. Or are we mistaken? I sometimes feel when I turn the pages of Sebastian's masterpiece that the "absolute solution" is there, somewhere, concealed in some passage I have read too hastily, or that it is intertwined with other words whose familiar guise deceived me. I don't know any other book that gives one this special sensation, and perhaps this was the author's special intention.

I recall vividly the day when I saw *The Doubtful Asphodel* announced in an English paper. I had come across a copy of that paper in the lobby of a hotel in Paris, where I was waiting for a man whom my firm wanted wheedled into settling a certain deal. I am not good at wheedling, and generally the business seemed to me less promising than it seemed to my employers. And as I sat there alone in the lugubriously comfortable hall, and read the publisher's advertisement and Sebastian's handsome black name in block letters, I envied his lot more acutely than I had ever envied it before. I did not know where he was at the time, I had not seen him for at least six years, nor did I know of his being so ill and so miserable. On the contrary, that announcement of his book seemed to me a token of happiness—and I imagined him standing in a warm cheerful room at some club, with his hands in his pockets, his ears glowing, his eyes moist and bright, a smile fluttering on his lips,—and all the other people in the room standing round him, holding glasses of port, and laughing at his jokes. It was a silly picture, but it kept shining in its trembling pattern of white shirtfronts and black dinner jackets and mellow-coloured wine, and clear-cut faces, as one of those coloured photographs you see on the back of magazines. I decided to get that book as soon as it was published, I always used to get his books at once, but somehow I was particularly impatient to get this one. Presently the person I was waiting for came down. He was an Englishman, and fairly well-read. As we talked for a few moments about ordinary things before broaching the business in hand, I pointed casually to the advertisement in the paper and asked whether he had read any of Sebastian Knight's books. He said he had read one or two—*The Prismatic Something* and *Lost Property*. I asked him whether he had liked them. He said he had in a way, but the author seemed to him a terrible snob, intellectually, at least. Asked to explain, he added that Knight seemed to him to be constantly playing some game of his own invention, without telling his partners its rules. He said he preferred books that made one think, and Knight's books didn't,—they left you puzzled and cross. Then he talked of another living author, whom he thought

181

so much better than Knight. I took advantage of a pause to enter on our business conversation. It did not prove as successful as my firm had expected.

The Doubtful Asphodel obtained many reviews, and most of them were long and quite flattering. But here and there the hint kept recurring that the author was a tired author, which seemed another way of saying that he was just an old bore. I even caught a faint suggestion of commiseration, as if *they* knew certain sad dreary things about the author which were not really in the book, but which permeated their attitude towards it. One critic even went as far as to say that he read it "with mingled feelings, because it was a rather unpleasant experience for the reader, to sit beside a deathbed and never be quite sure whether the author was the doctor or the patient." Nearly all the reviews gave to understand that the book was a little too long, and that many passages were obscure and obscurely aggravating. All praised Sebastian Knight's "sincerity"—whatever that was. I wondered what Sebastian thought of those reviews.

I lent my copy to a friend who kept it several weeks without reading it, and then lost it in a train. I got another and never lent it to anybody. Yes, I think that of all his books this is my favourite one. I don't know whether it makes one "think," and I don't much care if it does not. I like it for its own sake. I like its manners. And sometimes I tell myself that it would not be inordinately hard to translate it into Russian.

I HAVE managed to reconstruct more
or less the last year of Sebastian's life: 1935. He died in
the very beginning of 1936, and as I look at this figure I cannot help thinking that there is an occult resemblance between
a man and the date of his death. Sebastian Knight d. 1936 . . .
This date to me seems the reflection of that name in a pool of
rippling water. There is something about the curves of the
last three numerals that recalls the sinuous outlines of Sebastian's personality . . . I am trying, as I have often tried in
the course of this book, to express an idea that might have
appealed to him . . . If here and there I have not captured at
least the shadow of his thought, or if now and then unconscious cerebration has not led me to take the right turn in his
private labyrinth, then my book is a clumsy failure.

The appearance of *The Doubtful Asphodel* in the spring
of 1935 coincided with Sebastian's last attempt to see Nina.
When he was told by one of her sleek-haired young ruffians
that she wished to be rid of him for ever, he returned to London and stayed there for a couple of months, making a piti-
ful effort to deceive solitude by appearing in public as much
as he could. A thin, mournful and silent figure, he would be
seen in this place or that, wearing a scarf round his neck
even in the warmest dining-room, exasperating hostesses by
his absent-mindedness and his gentle refusal to be drawn
out, wandering away in the middle of a party, or being dis-

covered in the nursery, engrossed in a jigsaw-puzzle. One day, near Charing Cross, Helen Pratt saw Clare into a bookshop, and a few seconds later, as she was continuing her way, she ran into Sebastian. He coloured slightly as he shook hands with Miss Pratt, and then accompanied her to the underground station. She was thankful he had not appeared a minute earlier, and still more thankful when he did not trouble to allude to the past. He told her instead an elaborate story about a couple of men who had attempted to swindle him at a game of poker the night before.

"Glad to have met you," he said as they parted. "I think I shall get it here."

"Get what?" asked Miss Pratt.

"I was on my way to [he named the bookshop], but I see I can get what I want at this stall."

He went to concerts and plays, and drank hot milk in the middle of the night at coffee stalls with taxi drivers. He is said to have been three times to see the same film—a perfectly insipid one called *The Enchanted Garden*. A couple of months after his death, and a few days after I had learnt who Madame Lecerf really was, I discovered that film in a French cinema where I sat through the performance, with the sole intent of learning why it had attracted him so. Somewhere in the middle the story shifted to the Riviera, and there was a glimpse of bathers basking in the sun. Was Nina among them? Was it her naked shoulder? I thought that one girl who glanced back at the camera looked rather like her, but sun-oil and sun tan, and an eye-shade are much too good at disguising a passing face. He was very ill for a week in August, but he refused to take to his bed, as Doctor Oates prescribed. In September, he went to see some people in the country: he was but very slightly acquainted with them; and they had invited him out of mere politeness, because he happened to have said he had seen the picture of their house in the *Prattler*. For a whole week he wandered about a coldish house where all the other guests knew one another intimately, and then one morning he walked ten miles to the station and quietly travelled back to town, leaving dinner jacket and sponge-bag behind. In the beginning of November, he had lunch with Sheldon at Sheldon's club and was so taciturn that his friend wondered why he had come at all. Then comes a blank. Apparently he went abroad, but I hardly believe that he had any definite plan about trying to meet Nina again, though perhaps some faint hope of that kind was at the source of his restlessness.

I had spent most of the winter of 1935 in Marseilles, attending to some of my firm's business. In the middle of January, 1936, I got a letter from Sebastian. Strangely enough, it was written in Russian.

"I am, as you see, in Paris, and presumably shall be stuck [*zasstrianoo*] here for some time. If you can come, come; if you can't, I shall not be offended; but it might be perhaps better if you came. I am fed up [*osskominu*] with a number of tortuous things and especially with the patterns of my shed snake-skins [*vypolziny*] so that now I find a poetic solace in the obvious and the ordinary which for some reason or other I had overlooked in the course of my life. I should like for example to ask you what you have been doing during all these years, and to tell you about myself: I hope you have done better than I. Lately I have been seeing a good deal of old Dr. Starov, who treated *maman* [so Sebastian called my mother]. I met him by chance one night in the street, when I

185

was taking a forced rest on the running-board of somebody's parked car. He seemed to think that I had been vegetating in Paris since *maman's* death, and I have agreed to his version of my emigré existence, because [*eeboh*] any explanation seemed to me far too complicated. Some day you may come upon certain papers; you will burn them at once; true, they have heard voices in [one or two indecipherable words: *Dot chetu?*], but now they must suffer the stake. I kept them, and gave them night-lodgings [*notchleg*], because it is safer to let such things sleep, lest, when killed, they haunt us as ghosts. One night, when I felt particularly mortal, I signed their death-warrant, and by it you will know them. I had been staying at the same hotel as usual, but now I have moved to a kind of sanatorium out of town, note the address. This letter was begun almost a week ago, and up to the word 'life' it had been destined [*prednaznachalos*] to quite a different person. Then somehow or other it turned towards you, as a shy guest in a strange house will talk at unusual length to the near relative with whom he came to the party. So forgive me if I bore you [*dokoochayou*], but somehow I don't much like those bare branches and twigs which I see from my window."

This letter upset me, of course, but it did not make me as anxious as I should have been, had I known that since 1926 Sebastian had been suffering from an incurable disease, growing steadily worse during the last five years. I must shamefully confess that my natural alarm was somewhat subdued by the thought that Sebastian was very high-strung and nervous and had always been inclined to undue pessimism when his health was impaired. I had, I repeat, not the smallest inkling of his heart-trouble, and so I managed to convince myself that he was suffering from overwork. Still, he was ill and begging me to come in a tone that was novel to me. He had never seemed to need my presence, but now he was positively pleading for it. It moved me, and it puzzled me, and I would certainly have jumped into the very first train had I known the whole truth. I got the letter on Thursday and at once resolved to go to Paris on Saturday, so as to journey back on Sunday night, for I felt that my firm would not expect me to take a holiday at the critical stage of the business I was supposed to be looking after in Marseilles. I decided that instead of writing and explaining I would send him a telegram Saturday morning, when I should know whether, perhaps, I could take the earlier train.

And that night I dreamt a singularly unpleasant dream. I dreamt I was sitting in a large dim room which my dream had hastily furnished with odds and ends collected in different houses I vaguely knew, but with gaps or strange substitutions, as for instance that shelf which was at the same time a dusty road. I had a hazy feeling that the room was in a farmhouse or a country-inn—a general impression of wooden walls and planking. We were expecting Sebastian—he was due to come back from some long journey. I was sitting on a crate or something, and my mother was also in the room, and there were two more persons drinking tea at the table round which we were seated—a man from my office and his wife, both of whom Sebastian had never known, and who had been placed there by the dream-manager—just because anybody would do to fill the stage.

Our wait was uneasy, laden with obscure forebodings, and I felt that they knew more than I, but I dreaded to inquire why my mother worried so much about a muddy bicycle which refused to be crammed into the wardrobe: its doors kept opening. There was the picture of a steamer on the wall, and the waves on the picture moved like a procession of caterpillars, and the steamer rocked and this annoyed me—until I remembered that the hanging of such a picture was an old and commonplace custom, when awaiting a traveller's return. He might arrive at any moment, and the wooden floor near the door had been sprinkled with sand, so that he might not slip. My mother wandered away with the muddy spurs and stirrups she could not hide, and the vague couple was quietly abolished, for I was alone in the room, when a door opened in a gallery upstairs, and Sebastian appeared, slowly descending a rickety flight of stairs which came straight down into the room. His hair was tousled and he was coatless: he had, I understood, just been taking a nap after his journey. As he came down, pausing a little on every step, with always the same foot ready to continue and with his arm resting on the wooden hand-rail, my mother came back again and helped him to get up when he stumbled and slithered down on his back. He laughed as he came up to me, but I felt that he was ashamed of something. His face was pale and unshaven, but it looked fairly cheerful. My mother, with a silver cup in her hand, sat down on what proved to be a stretcher, for she was presently carried away by two men who slept on Saturdays in the house, as Sebastian told me with a smile. Suddenly I noticed that he wore a black glove on his left hand, and that the fingers of that hand did not move, and that he never used it—I was afraid horribly, squeamishly, to the point of nausea, that he might inadvertently touch me with it, for I understood now that it was a sham thing attached to the wrist,—that he had been operated upon, or had had some dreadful accident. I understood too why his appearance and the whole atmosphere of his arrival seemed so uncanny, but though he perhaps noticed my shudder, he went on with his tea. My mother came back for a moment to fetch the thimble she had forgotten and quickly went away, for the men were in a hurry. Sebastian asked me whether the manicurist had already come, as he was anxious to get ready for the banquet. I tried to dismiss the subject, because the idea of his maimed hand was insufferable, but presently I saw the whole room in terms of jagged fingernails, and a girl I had known (but she had strangely faded now) arrived with her manicure case and sat down on a stool in front of Sebastian. He asked me not to look, but I could not help looking. I saw him undoing his black glove and slowly pulling it off; and as it came off, it spilt its only contents—a number of tiny hands, like the front paws of a mouse, mauve-pink and soft,—lots of them,—and they dropped to the floor, and the girl in black went on her knees. I bent down to see what she was doing under the table and I saw that she was picking up the little hands and putting them into a dish,—I looked up and Sebastian had vanished, and when I bent down again, the girl had vanished too. I felt I could not stay in that room for a moment longer. But as I turned and groped for the latch I heard Sebastian's voice behind me; it seemed to come from the darkest and remotest corner of what was now an enormous barn with grain trickling out of a punctured bag at my feet. I could not see him and was so eager to escape that the throbbing of my impatience seemed to drown the words he said. I knew he was calling me and saying something very important—and promising to tell me something more important still, if only I came to the corner where he sat or lay, trapped by the heavy sacks that had fallen across his legs. I moved, and then his voice came in one last loud insistent appeal, and a phrase which made no sense when I brought it out of my dream, then, in the dream itself, rang out laden with such absolute moment, with such an unfailing intent to solve for me a monstrous riddle, that I would have run to Sebastian after all, had I not been half out of my dream already.

I know that the common pebble you find in your fist after having thrust your arm shoulder deep into water, where a jewel seemed to gleam on pale sand, is really the coveted gem though it looks like a pebble as it dries in the sun of everyday. Therefore I felt that the nonsensical sentence which sang in my head as I awoke was really the garbled translation of a striking disclosure; and as I lay on my back listening to the familiar sounds in the street and to the inane musical hash of the wireless brightening somebody's early breakfast in the room above my head, the prickly cold of some dreadful apprehension produced an almost physical shudder in me and I decided to send a wire telling Sebastian I was coming that very day. Owing to some idiotic piece of commonsense (which otherwise was never my forte), I thought I'd better find out at the Marseilles branch of my office whether my presence might be spared. I discovered that not only it might not, but that it was doubtful whether I could absent myself at all for the weekend. That Friday I came home very late after a harassing day. There was a telegram waiting for me since noon,—but so strange is the sovereignty of daily platitudes over the delicate revelations of a dream that I had quite forgotten its earnest whisper, and was simply expecting some business news as I burst the telegram open.

"Sevastian's state hopeless come immediately Starov." It

was worded in French; the "v" in Sebastian's name was a transcription of its Russian spelling; for some reason unknown, I went to the bathroom and stood there for a moment in front of the looking-glass. Then I snatched my hat and ran downstairs. The time was a quarter to twelve when I reached the station, and there was a train at 0.02, arriving at Paris about half past two p.m. on the following day.

Then I discovered that I had not enough cash about me to afford a second-class ticket, and for a minute I debated with myself the question whether generally it would not be better to go back for some more and fly to Paris as soon as I could get a plane. But the train's near presence proved too tempting. I took the cheapest opportunity, as I usually do in life. And no sooner had the train moved than I realised with a shock that I had left Sebastian's letter in my desk and did not remember the address he had given.

THE crowded compartment was dark, stuffy and full of legs. Rain drops trickled down the panes: they did not trickle straight but in a jerky, dubious, zig-zag course, pausing every now and then. The violet-blue night-lamp was reflected in the black glass. The train rocked and groaned as it rushed through the night. What on earth was the name of that sanitorium? It began with an "M." It began with an "M." It began with an . . . the wheels got mixed up in their repetitive rush and then found their rhythm again. Of course, I would obtain the address from Doctor Starov. Ring him up from the station as soon as I arrived. Somebody's heavily-booted dream tried to get in between my shins and then was slowly withdrawn. What had Sebastian meant by "the usual hotel?" I could not re-call any special place in Paris where he had stayed. Yes, Starov would know where he was. Mar . . . Man . . . Mat . . . Would I get there in time? My neighbor's hip pushed at mine, as he switched from one kind of snore to another, sadder one. Would I arrive in time to find him alive . . . arrive . . . alive . . . arrive . . . He had something to tell me, something of boundless importance. The dark, rock-ing compartment, chock-full of sprawling dummies, seemed to me a section of the dream I had had. What would he tell me before he died? The rain spat and tinkled against the glass and a ghost-like snowflake settled in one corner and melted away. Somebody in front of me slowly came to life; rustled paper and munched in the dark, and then lit a cigarette, and its round glow stared at me like a Cyclopean eye. I must, I must get there in time. Why had I not dashed to the aerodrome as soon as I got that letter? I would have been with Sebastian by now! What was the illness he was dying of? Cancer? Angina pectoris—like his mother? As it happens with many people who do not trouble about religion in the ordinary trend of life, I hastily invented a soft, warm, tear-misty God, and whispered an informal prayer. Let me get there in time, let him hold out till I come, let him tell me his secret. Now it was all snow: the glass had grown a grey beard. The man who had munched and smoked was asleep again. Could I try and stretch out my legs, and put my feet up on something? I groped with my burning toes, but the night was all bone and flesh. I yearned in vain for a wooden something under my ankles and calves. Mar ... Matamar ... Mar ... How far was that place from Paris? Doctor Starov. Alexander Alexandrovich Starov. The train clattered over the points, repeating those x's. Some unknown station. As the train stopped voices came from the next compartment, somebody was telling an endless tale. There was also the shifting sound of doors being moved aside, and some mournful traveller drew our door open too, and saw it was hopeless. Hopeless. *Etat désespéré*. I must get there in time. How long that train stopped at stations! My righthand neighbour sighed and tried to wipe the window-pane, but it remained misty with a faint yellowish light glimmering through. The train moved on again. My spine ached, my bones were leaden. I tried to shut my eyes and to doze, but my eyelids were lined with floating designs—and a tiny bundle of light, rather like an infusoria, swam across, starting again from the same corner. I seemed to recognise in it the shape of the station lamp which had passed by long ago. Then colours appeared, and a pink face with a large gazelle eye slowly turned towards me—and then a basket of flowers, and then Sebastian's unshaven chin. I could not stand that optical paintbox any longer, and with endless, cautious manoeuvering, resembling the steps of some ballet dancer filmed in slow motion, I got out into the corridor. It was brightly lit and cold. For a time I smoked and then staggered towards the end of the carriage, and swayed for a moment over a filthy roaring hole in the train's bottom, and staggered back, and smoked another cigarette. Never in my life had I wanted a thing as fiercely as I wanted to find Sebastian alive,—to bend over him and catch the words he would say. His last book, my recent dream, the mysteriousness of his letter—all made me firmly believe that some extraordinary revelation would come from his lips. If I found them still moving. If I were not too late. There was a map on the panel between the windows, but it had nothing to do with the course of my journey. My face was darkly reflected in the window-pane. *Il est dangereux* . . . *E pericoloso* . . . a soldier with red eyes brushed past me and for some seconds a horrible tingle remained in my hand, because it had touched his sleeve. I craved for a wash. I longed to wash the coarse world away and appear in a cold aura of purity before Sebastian. He had done with mortality now and I could not offend his nostrils with its reek. Oh, I would find him alive. Starov would not have worded his telegram that way, had he been sure that I would be late. The telegram had come at noon. The telegram, my God, had come at noon! Sixteen hours had already passed, and when

might I reach Mar . . . Mat . . . Ram . . . Rat . . . No, not "R"—
it began with an "M." For a moment I saw the dim shape of
the name, but it faded before I could grasp it. And there might
be another setback: money. I should dash from the station to
my office and get some at once. The office was quite near.
The bank was farther. Did anybody of my numerous friends
live near the station? No, they all lived in Passy or around
the Porte St. Cloud,—the two Russian quarters of Paris. I
squashed my third cigarette and looked for a less crowded
compartment. There was, thank God, no luggage to keep me
in the one I had left. But the carriage was crammed and I was
much too sick in mind to go down the train. I am not even
sure whether the compartment into which I groped, was another or the old one: it was just as full of knees and feet and
elbows—though perhaps the air was a little less cheesy.
Why had I never visited Sebastian in London? He had invited me once or twice. Why had I kept away from him so
stubbornly, when he was the man I admired most of all men?
Those bloody asses who sneered at his genius . . . There was,
in particular, one old fool whose skinny neck I longed to
wring—ferociously. Ah, that bulky monster rolling on my
left was a woman; eau-de-Cologne and sweat struggling for
ascendancy, the former losing. Not a single soul in that carriage knew who Sebastian Knight was. That chapter out of
Lost Property so poorly translated in *Cadran*. Or was it *La
Vie Littéraire*? Or was I too late, too late—was Sebastian
dead already, while I sat on this accursed bench with a de-
risive bit of thin leather padding which could not deceive
my aching buttocks? Faster, please faster! Why do you
think it worth stopping at this station? and why stop so long?
Move, move on. So—that's better.

Very gradually the darkness faded to a greyish dimness, and a snow-covered world became faintly perceptible through the window. I felt dreadfully cold in my thin raincoat. The faces of my travelling companions became visible as if layers of webs and dust were slowly brushed away. The woman next to me had a thermos flask of coffee and she handled it with a kind of maternal love. I felt sticky all over and excruciatingly unshaven. I think that if my bristly cheek had come into contact with satin, I should have fainted. There was a flesh-coloured cloud among the drab ones, and a dull pink flushed the patches of thawing snow in the tragic loneliness of barren fields. A road drew out and glided for a minute along the train, and just before it turned away a man on a bicycle wobbled among snow and slush and puddles. Where was he going? Who was he? Nobody will ever know.

I think I must have dozed for an hour or so—or at least I managed to keep my inner vision dark. My companions were talking and eating when I opened my eyes and I suddenly felt so sick that I scrambled out and sat on a strapontin for the rest of the journey, my mind as blank as the wretched morning. The train, I learnt, was very late, owing to the night blizzard or something, so it was only at a quarter to four in the afternoon that we reached Paris. My teeth chattered as I walked down the platform and for an instant I had a foolish impulse to spend the two or three francs jingling in my pocket on some strong liquor. But I went to the telephone instead. I thumbed the soft greasy book, looking for Dr. Starov's number and trying not to think that presently I should know whether Sebastian was still alive. Starkaus, cuirs, peaux; Starley, jongleur, humoriste; Starov . . . ah, there it was.: Jasmin 61-93. I performed some dreadful manipulations and forgot the number in the middle, and struggled again with the book, and re-dialled, and listened for a while to an ominous buzzing. I sat for a minute quite still: somebody threw the door open and with an angry muttering retreated. Again the dial turned and clicked back, five, six, seven times, and again there was that nasal drone: donne, donne, donne . . . Why was I so unlucky? "Have you finished?" asked the same person—a cross old man with a bulldog face. My nerves were on edge and I quarreled with that nasty old fellow. Fortunately a neighbouring booth was free by now; he slammed himself in. I went on trying. At last I succeeded. A woman's voice replied that the doctor was out, but could be reached at half past five,—she gave me the number. When I got to my office I could not help noticing that my arrival provoked a certain surprise. I showed the telegram I had got to my chief and he was less sympathetic than one might have reasonably expected. He asked me some awkward questions about the business in Marseilles. Finally I got the money I wanted and paid the taxi which I had left at the door. It was twenty minutes to five by then so that I had almost an hour before me.

I went to have a shave and then ate a hurried breakfast. At twenty past five I rang up the number I had been given, and was told that the doctor had gone home and would be back in a quarter of an hour. I was too impatient to wait and dialled his home number. The female voice I already knew answered that he had just left. I leant against the wall (the booth was in a café this time) and knocked at it with my pencil. Would I never get to Sebastian? Who were those idle idiots who wrote on the wall "Death to the Jews" or *"Vive le front populaire,"* or left obscene drawings? Some anonymous artist had begun blacking squares—a chess board, *ein*

Schachbrett, un damier . . . There was a flash in my brain and the word settled on my tongue: St. Damier! I rushed out and hailed a passing taxicab. Would he take me to St. Damier, wherever the place was? He leisurely unfolded a map and studied it for some time. Then he replied that it would take two hours at least to get there—seeing the condition of the road. I asked him whether he thought I had better go by train. He did not know.

"Well, try and go fast," I said, and knocked my hat off as I plunged into the car.

We were a long time getting out of Paris. Every kind of known obstacle was put in our way, and I think I have never hated anything so much as I did a certain policeman's arm at one of the crossroads. At last we wriggled out of the traffic jam into a long dark avenue. But still we did not go fast enough. I pushed the glass open and implored the chauffeur to increase his speed. He answered that the road was far too slippery—as it was we badly skidded once or twice. After an hour's drive he stopped and asked his way of a policeman on a bicycle. They both pored at length over the policeman's map, and then the chauffeur drew his own out, and they compared both. We had taken a wrong turning somewhere and now had to go back for at least a couple of miles. I tapped again on the pane: the taxi was positively crawling. He shook his head without as much as turning round. I looked at my watch, it was nearing seven o'clock. We stopped at a filling-station and the driver had a confidential talk with the garage man. I could not guess where we were, but as the road now ran along a vast expanse of fields, I hoped that we were getting nearer my goal. Rain swept and swished against the window-panes and when I pleaded once more with the driver for a little acceleration, he lost his temper and was volubly rude. I felt helpless and numb as I sank back in my seat. Lighted windows blurredly passed by. Would I ever get to Sebastian? Would I find him alive if I did ever reach St. Damier? Once or twice we were overtaken by other cars and I drew my driver's attention to their speed. He did not answer, but suddenly stopped and with a violent gesture unfolded his ridiculous map. I inquired whether he had lost his way again. He kept silent but the expression of his fat neck was vicious. We drove on. I noticed with satisfaction that he was going much faster now. We passed under a railway bridge and drew up at a station. As I was wondering whether it was St. Damier at last, the driver got out of his seat and wrenched open the door. "Well," I asked, "what's the matter now?"

"You shall go by train after all," said the driver, "I'm not willing to smash my car for your sake. This is the St. Damier line, and you're lucky to have been brought here."

I was even luckier than he thought for there was a train in a few minutes. The station-guard swore I would be at St. Damier by nine. That last phase of my journey was the darkest. I was alone in the carriage and a queer torpor had seized me: in spite of my impatience, I was terribly afraid lest I might fall asleep and miss the station. The train stopped often and it was every time a sickening task to find and decipher the station's name. At one stage I experienced the hideous feeling that I had just been jerked awake after dozing heavily for an unknown length of time—and when I looked at my watch it was a quarter past nine. Had I missed it? I was half-inclined to use the alarm signal, but then I felt the train was slowing down, and as I leant out of the window, I espied a lighted sign floating past and stopping: St. Damier.

A quarter of an hour's stumble through dark lanes and what seemed by its sough to be a pine-wood, brought me to the St. Damier hospital. I heard a shuffling and wheezing behind the door and a fat old man clad in a thick grey sweater instead of a coat and in worn felt slippers let me in. I entered a kind of office dimly lit by a weak bare electric lamp, which seemed coated with dust on one side. The man looked at me blinking, his bloated face glistening with the slime of sleep, and for some odd reason I spoke at first in a whisper.

"I have come," I said, "to see Monsieur Sebastian Knight, K, n, i, g, h, t. Knight. Night."

He grunted and sat down heavily at a writing-desk under the hanging lamp.

"Too late for visitors," he mumbled as if talking to himself.

"I got a wire," I said, "my brother is very ill,"—and as I spoke I felt I was trying to imply that there was not the shade of a doubt of Sebastian still being alive.

"What was the name?" he asked with a sigh.

"Knight," I said. "It begins with a 'K'. It is an English name."

"Foreign names ought to be always replaced by numbers," muttered the man, "it would simplify matters. There was a patient who died last night, and he had a name . . ."

I was struck by the horrible thought that he might be referring to Sebastian . . . Was I too late after all?

"Do you mean to say . . ." I began, but he shook his head and turned the pages of a ledger on his desk.

"No," he growled, "the English Monsieur is not dead. K, K, K . . ."

"K, n, i, g . . ." I began once again.

"C'est bon, c'est bon," he interrupted. "K, n, K, g . . . n . . . I'm not an idiot, you know. Number thirty-six."

He rang the bell and sank back in his armchair with a yawn. I paced up and down the room in a tremor of uncontrollable impatience. At last a nurse entered and the night-porter pointed at me.

"Number thirty-six," he said to the nurse.

I followed her down a white passage and up a short flight of stairs. "How is he?" I could not help asking.

"I don't know," she said and led me to a second nurse who was sitting at the end of another white passage, the exact copy of the first, and reading a book at a little table.

"A visitor for number thirty-six," said my guide and slipped away.

"But the English Monsieur is asleep," said the nurse, a round-faced young woman, with a very small and very shiny nose.

"Is he better?" I asked. "You see, I'm his brother, and I got a telegram . . ."

"I think he's a little better," said the nurse with a smile, which was to me the loveliest smile I could have ever imagined.

"He had a very, very bad heart attack yesterday morning. Now he is asleep."

"Look here," I said, handing her a ten or twenty franc coin. I'll come to-morrow again, but I'd like to go into his room and wait for a minute there."

"Oh, but you shouldn't wake him," she said smiling again.

"I shan't wake him. I shall just sit near him and stay only a minute."

"Well, I don't know," she said. "You might, of course, peep in here, but you must be very careful."

She led me to the door, Number thirty-six, and we entered a tiny room or closet with a couch; she pushed slightly an inner door which was standing ajar and I peered for a moment into a dark room. At first I could only hear my heart thumping, but then I discerned a quick soft breathing. I strained my eyes; there was a screen or something half round the bed, and anyway it would have been too dark to distinguish Sebastian.

"There," whispered the nurse. "I shall leave the door open an inch and you may sit here, on this couch, for a minute."

She lit a small blue-shaded lamp and left me alone. I had a stupid impulse to draw my cigarette case out of my pocket. My hands still shook, but I felt happy. He was alive. He was peacefully asleep. So it was his heart—was it?—that had let him down . . . The same as his mother. He was better, there was hope. I would get all the heart specialists in the world to have him saved. His presence in the next room, the faint sound of breathing, gave me a sense of security, of peace, of wonderful relaxation. And as I sat there and listened, and clasped my hands, I thought of all the years that had passed, of our short, rare meetings and I knew that now, as soon as he could listen to me, I should tell him that whether he liked it or not I would never be far from him any more. The strange dream I had had, the belief in some momentous truth he would impart to me before dying—now seemed vague, abstract, as if it had been drowned in some warm flow of simpler, more human emotion, in the wave of love I felt for the man who was sleeping beyond that half-opened door. How had we managed to drift apart? Why had I always been so silly and sullen, and shy during our short interviews in Paris? I would go away presently and spend the night in the hotel, or perhaps they could give me a room at the hospital—just until I could see him? For a moment it seemed to me that the faint rhythm of the sleeper's breath had been suspended, that he had awaked and made a light champing sound, before sinking again into sleep: now the rhythm continued, so low that I could hardly distinguish it from my own breath, as I sat and listened. Oh, I would tell him thousands of things —I would talk to him about *The Prismatic Bezel* and *Success*, and *The Funny Mountain*, and *Albinos in Black*, and *The Back of the Moon*, and *Lost Property*, and *The Doubtful Asphodel*,—all these books that I knew as well as if I had written them myself. And he would talk, too. How little I knew of his life! But now I was learning something every instant. That door standing slightly ajar was the best link imaginable. That gentle breathing was telling me more of Sebastian than I had ever known before. If I could have smoked, my happiness would have been perfect. A spring clanked in the couch as I shifted my position slightly, and I was afraid that it might have disturbed his sleep. But no: the soft sound was there, following a thin trail which seemed to skirt time itself, now dipping into a hollow, now appearing again,— steadily travelling across a landscape formed of the symbols of silence—darkness, and curtains, and a glow of blue light at my elbow.

Presently I got up and tiptoed out into the corridor.

"I hope," the nurse said, "you did not disturb him? It is good that he sleeps."

"Tell me," I asked, "when does Doctor Starov come?"

"Doctor who?" she said. "Oh, the Russian doctor. *Non, c'est le docteur Guinet qui le soigne.* You'll find him here to-morrow morning."

"You see," I said, "I'd like to spend the night somewhere here. Do you think that perhaps . . ."

"You could see Doctor Guinet even now," continued the nurse in her quiet pleasant voice. "He lives next door. So you are the brother, are you? And to-morrow his mother is coming from England, n'est-ce pas?"

"Oh, no," I said, "his mother died years ago. And tell me, how is he during the day, does he talk? does he suffer?"

She frowned and looked at me queerly.

"But . . ." she said. "I don't understand . . . What is your name, please?"

"Right," I said. "I haven't explained. We are half-brothers, really. My name is [I mentioned my name]."

"Oh-la-la!" she exclaimed getting very red in the face. "Mon Dieu! The Russian gentleman died yesterday, and you've been visiting Monsieur Kegan . . ."

So I did not see Sebastian after all, or at least I did not see him alive. But those few minutes I spent listening to what I thought was his breathing changed my life as completely as it would have been changed, had Sebastian spoken to me before dying. Whatever his secret was, I have learnt one secret too, and namely: that the soul is but a manner of being—not a constant state—that any soul may be yours, if you find and follow its undulations. The hereafter may be the full ability of consciously living in any chosen soul, in any number of souls, all of them unconscious of their interchangeable burden. Thus—I am Sebastian Knight. I feel as if I were impersonating him on a lighted stage, with the people he knew coming and going—the dim figures of the few friends he had, the scholar, and the poet, and the painter,—smoothly and noiselessly paying their graceful tribute; and here is Goodman, the flat-footed buffoon, with his dicky hanging out of his waistcoat; and there—the pale radiance of Clare's inclined head, as she is led away weeping by a friendly maiden. They move round Sebastian—round me who am acting Sebastian,—and the old conjuror waits in the wings with his hidden rabbit; and Nina sits on a table in the brightest corner of the stage, with a wineglass of fuchsined water, under a painted palm. And then the masquerade draws to a close. The bald little prompter shuts his book, as the light fades gently. The end, the end. They all go back to their everyday life (and Clare goes back to her grave)—but the hero remains, for, try as I may, I cannot get out of my part: Sebastian's mask clings to my face, the likeness will not be washed off. I am Sebastian, or Sebastian is I, or perhaps we both are someone whom neither of us knows.

THE END